THE LOST BOYS
OF LAMPSON

The Vancouver Island Mysteries Series, Volume 2
By P.N. Holland

Filidh Publishing

Copyright © 2023 P.N. Holland (Revised Edition)
ISBN 978-1-927848-76-0
Filidh Publishing, Victoria, BC
Revised Cover Design by Danny Weeds.
Original Front Cover Art © 2014 Celairen
Back cover photo credit: iStockphoto ID: 512250305 Credit: imijaloff

Third Copyright © March 5, 2020, P.N. Holland
Second Copyright 2017© P.N. Holland
ISBN 978-1-77127-918-5
ISBN 978-1-77127-566-8 eBook
MuseItUp Publishing
Original Copyright © 2014 by Peter Neil Holland

 Also, by P.N. Holland
The Vancouver Island Mysteries Series:
      The Saxe Point Park Mystery, Volume 1
      The E&N Escape, Volume 3
Vahldohr: Mellissadorha Series – Book One
      Watch for more at https://pnholland.com/.

****

This story is dedicated to the patience, support and interest shown by my late wife, Kris, and to our grandchildren, who will continue to enjoy my writing.

****

Acknowledgements

Thanks to Bev Cooke, my former editor, mentor, and friend, for her support, help, and belief in my craft.

****

CHAPTER ONE

Dark Start

Billy walked onto the grounds of Lampson Street School, and the hair on the back of his neck prickled. Lampson was warm, inviting, and comfortable, but not this morning. The quiet was unnatural. Hesitating, he turned, but the school ground was empty. Shivers ran down his spine as he gazed up at the bell tower. *Nope, no ghoul gawking down at me.* He snickered, dropped his backpack on the steps, and studied the red brick building. As always, the tall red walls, shiny steel roof, and grey stone steps met his gaze, but he shuddered at its cold, somewhat sphinxlike indifference. The red doors sat like a mouth ready to swal- low the kids returning from summer holidays.

The cawing of crows collecting on the eaves distracted him. More and more of them landed on the silver metal, clicking and clacking along its surface in a weird dance. Even though the sun shone, a chill ran through him as he stared at the top windows. The drawn blinds looked like closed eyelids below the bald sun's glare on the roof.

A shadowy form appeared at the one uncovered window, a stick in its hand or maybe a cane, the end glowing white. Frozen, Billy couldn't take his eyes off the bright orb as the dark figure of a man pointed it at him. The tip glowed like a torch exposing the white hair of the person behind it. Billy's head spun, his heart pounded, his vision blurred, and his knees buckled; he saw a dark place, a cold place. Only the crows' squawking kept him from passing out.

A voice penetrated. "What's with you?"

Billy staggered, shook his head, and turned around.

Ricky, his friend, grabbed his arm. "Are you okay, man?"

Billy sat down on the steps, his heart thumping. "I...think so."

Ricky leaned down. "You sure? I called you three times."

"Yeah, do you...see anything...in that open window?" Billy pointed.

"Nope. What did you see?"

Billy paused to catch his breath. "I saw a man in the window. He was holding a strange, glowing stick or something. I went dizzy and—"

"Really?" He patted Billy on the back. "I think the sun is getting to you, mate."

Billy's anger flared. "I know what I saw, *okay?*"

"Maybe it's the Ghost of Lampson. *Oooo.*" Ricky smiled and flapped his arms.

Billy's face flushed, his fists clenched. "I'm not kidding. I saw something."

"Take it easy, man." Ricky tapped him on the shoulder. "Maybe it's Max Maynard? They say he haunts the bell tower."

Billy frowned.

"What about that guy who fell through the sky- light years ago or that teacher who disappeared in the fifties? Remember? The librarian told us about them last year."

Billy took several deep breaths. "Those are just stories. This was real."

His friend nodded. "Okay, okay, I believe you. But it could've been something else like—"

"He was there. The cane and that glowing thing were there, too."

"What glowing thing?" Billy's sister Sarah asked as she and her friend, Mia, came up the stairs.

"Ah, nothing, Sarah." He struggled to sound casual and tried to get himself under control. "I just saw someone up in that window." He pointed.

"Like a ghost?" Sarah asked.

"Maybe," Ricky said.

"You saw a ghost?" Mia asked, her eyes wide.

"I don't know. Anyway, shouldn't you be lining up now? It's bell time." Billy changed the subject, not wanting everyone to think he was loony. He rubbed his arms and rolled his shoulders, trying to shake off the anger. He knew what he saw.

"Okay," Sarah said, "but we came to ask you about the grade three teachers."

Billy smiled."Let me see. It'll be Mrs. Morris or Ms. Longbottom. They're both nasty old bags." He winked at Ricky.

"Good one," Ricky said. He laughed and looked up toward the bell tower. The murder of crows cawed back.

"Billy MacLean, you're awful!" Sarah scolded. "Sally Sims says Ms. Longbottom is very nice." She grabbed Mia's arm. "Come on, Mia. Boys are impossible." They marched back down the stairs.

A bunch of other kids reached the bottom of the stairs."Maybe we should talk about this later," Ricky whispered. Billy nodded and grabbed his backpack.

Ms. Fenton, the principal, opened the big red doors and stepped out of the school. "Ah, Billy, Ricky, two grade sevens, what luck. Would you boys be the first to hold the doors this year?" she asked.

"I guess so," Billy answered. Ricky shrugged. They trudged over to the doors as the principal asked a grade one student to ring the bell. The little girl grinned and bounced up the stairs as if she'd just won the lottery. Billy gazed over the cement rail at the huge oak trees on the front lawn. Their gnarled trunks reminded him of old men, crusty branches swaying like wrinkled hands scratching the sky. Many were as old as Lampson, some even older. Their long, eerie shadows danced against the side of the school. A shiver ran down his spine.

The school buzzer rang, breaking his thoughts. The door slipped from his hand, slamming against the door frame. The noise startled the little girl, and she dropped the brass bell. It clanged, the girl scampering after it as it rolled down the stairs. At the bottom, an older girl stopped it and handed it to her. Billy rolled his eyes at Ricky, and they both giggled.

"It's okay," said Ms. Fenton. The little girl smiled as she swung the bell. It rang, and the students charged up the stairs from both sides.

"Slow down, slow down!" Ms. Fenton yelled, but the kids ignored her. Billy leaned against the door, watching them stream by as a cold wind burst out of the school, almost knocking him over.

7

Shivering, his hair in his face, his clothes flapping, he grabbed the door with both hands and glanced at Ricky, who leaned against the door, his arms crossed, staring back.

"Can't you feel that?" Billy yelled. Ricky grimaced but continued to stare. "Hey, can't you hear me?" He slipped but grabbed the door as his hat blew off his head. "Your hat!" Billy hollered, but his friend only glanced at where it landed against the cement wall as the kids marched past. "Am I invisible or something?" Billy shouted into the wind. Nobody answered. "Ah-hh!" he screamed just as the wind stopped, leaving him slumped against the door.

Ricky jumped up. "You okay, man?"

Ms. Fenton raised her eyebrows; the kids stopped and stared as Billy blushed, snickered, and grabbed his finger. "Uh, I pinched my finger," he said. It was the only thing he could think of, and when everyone had filed in, the boys closed the doors. "You must have felt that wind!" Billy said.

"Gotta get my hat," Ricky said as he hopped across the cement to grab it.

"Come on, man. I know you did." Billy wasn't letting it go.

"So? It was just the wind."

"Yeah, but it came from inside."

"Maybe a window was open. Let's get inside before it blows again." He grabbed his pack, opened the door, and dashed inside the school.

"I know you felt it, too," Billy said. He ran up the stairs where Ms. Overon met them. She glowered and pointed her finger toward the bottom. "Boys, you can just march back down those stairs and *walk* up this time. You're seniors now. You need to set an example."

"Yes, Ms. Overon," they chorused, used to her harping. *You can't get away with anything these days. She's the school rule cop, always nattering about manners and "proper decorum."*

When they reached the bottom of the stairs, a girl skipped out of the office. The boys nearly knocked her over.

"Sorry," they blurted.

She raised her head, smiled, and blinked her deep, green eyes. *Funny, none of the other girls dress like that in a skirt, blouse, and vest.*

"You're new, aren't you?" Ricky said.

"Yes, well, sort of," she said as she stepped onto the stairs.

"What do you mean, sort of ?" Billy asked, but before she could answer, Mr. Moore, the vice principal, told them to hurry to the gym.

"Here, let me show you the way," Ricky said and jumped ahead of her. She brushed past Billy, the wool of her vest rubbing against his hand, fuzzy and old-fashioned, unlike his sister's clothes, which were smooth and bright. *Maybe her parents shop at a vintage Value Village.*

"Welcome back, everybody, and a special Lampson welcome to the new students. I trust we all had a great summer, and we're ready to continue our learning..." Ms. Fenton was saying as they entered the gym.

"Yeah, welcome to another boring year of bullshit." A whispered comment from behind made them turn around. Andrew Edgeware smirked as he sat with a bunch of boys.

"...and don't forget, boys and girls, today is only a half day, so go straight home at lunch time," the principal continued.

"What are you losers looking at?" Andrew asked.

The boys around him laughed. Before they could answer, all of the open windows slammed shut. Billy jumped and looked around. Everyone stopped talking for a second as the room held its breath.

When the chattering resumed, it sounded like the nattering of the crows on the roof. In the babble, a little girl asked her mother, "Mom, can I go to another school? This one doesn't like us."

I don't think Lampson likes me either, thought Billy.

— CHAPTER TWO —

The Fight

In the classroom, Billy slumped down in his seat and gazed out the window at the trees. *Who was that face in the window? Why did the wind only affect Ricky and me? What's going on?*

Mr. Moore called attendance, "Christie Adams, Shane Berkholder..."

"More like butt holder," Andrew whispered. The boys laughed.

"Denise Cuthbert, Damen Darling, Andrew Edgeware, Frederick Feinstein..."

"You mean Farting Freddie," Andrew said. This time Billy and Ricky laughed, too. *Andrew is pretty funny sometimes.* The names droned on as he gazed back out the window. *Maybe it was a ghost I saw. What was with that glowing cane, though, and why did he point it at me?*

"Excuse me, sir." Billy's head snapped around. It was the new girl—blond hair, green eyes, and a skirt.

"Come in, my dear. What's your name?" Mr. Moore asked.

"Amy Sutherland, sir."

"Welcome, Amy. There's a seat for you right beside Joanna Jenkins. Joanna, help her with her things, would you?" Joanna jumped up and took Amy's books. "Use one of the spare hooks at the back, Amy."

She hung up her things and sat down beside Joanna, smiling across at Billy as she did. He smiled back and looked her over with her strange clothes and her hair in a bun. *She is different. Where did this kid come from? A hundred years ago? She is cute, though.*

"Who's the weird kid?" Andrew whispered.

"I don't know, man, but she sure wears goofy clothes," Damen, one of his buddies, whispered back.

"Yeah, she looks like Little Orphan Annie," Andrew said. All the boys giggled.

Billy gave him a dirty look. *What a smart ass.* "Keep your opinions to yourself," Ricky said.

"Yeah, leave her alone," Billy added.

Andrew laughed. "Oooo, the loser twins have a crush on her."

"Go figure," Damen said. A bunch of the kids laughed, and Mr. Moore scolded Andrew for his comment. Ricky scowled at them, and Billy shook his head. At recess, Billy stopped a fast kick from Jesse Tompkins and booted the soccer ball to Ricky, who slammed it back to him. He noticed a crowd forming over by the rocks. Someone in the middle was crying. "Leave me alone," a girl wailed. Billy frowned.

Voices rang out from the crowd. "You're weird. Where'd you come from? You don't belong here."

Whoever it is, she's in trouble. Distracted, Billy started when a ball smacked him in the head. He ignored it and jogged over to the commotion.

"Where're you going?" Ricky asked, running after him.

"Those kids are picking on someone," Billy said, pointing to the crowd. "I think I know who it is."

"Go back home to Mama. What a cry baby." The kids swayed back and forth, most of them laughing.

"What's going on?" Billy asked, pushing his way into the circle.

"Nothing, Billy. Little Miss Weirdo doesn't belong, that's all," Andrew said. "She's just a big crybaby." Billy gasped. He did know the voice; it was Amy's, and she whimpered as the kids teased her.

"Crybaby, crybaby."

"Yeah, go home, you big baby," Andrew said, picking up a stick.

"What are you doing, Andrew?" Billy stared.

"What do you care?" Andrew whacked the stick against his leg, making it snap like a whip. Amy jumped back, but the crowd blocked her escape.

"Is she your girlfriend?" Damen asked. The kids laughed.

"Crybaby and the loser twins," Andrew said. He swung the stick over his head. "Go figure." The kids roared.

"Come on, Amy," Billy offered her his hand.

"Yeah, come on, Amy," Andrew mimicked. His arm flashed out, and the stick thudded into the side of her head. She fell into the mud. The crowd went silent and backed up.

"Stop it, Andrew!" Billy yelled. He held his hand up and leaned over Amy.

Andrew swung the stick over Billy's head. "Whoa, what are you doing, man?" Damen asked. The crowd muttered, and an icy chill struck Billy's face. Andrew's eyes shone yellow and piercing like a wolf's.

"She asked for it. Whining like that. She's just a *wuss*."Andrew's voice sounded low, cold, and forceful, more like a man's voice. Andrew bent over and ripped her blouse. Amy cried and pulled her torn clothes together. Andrew laughed, grabbed Billy's shirt and threw him on top of Amy. "Bend down and give her a kiss, lover boy," he said. Billy slammed into her knees, losing his breath, his head bouncing off her chest. Amy cried out in agony.

"Andrew, stop it," Ricky shouted and stepped for- ward.

"Back off, loser." Andrew shoved him and raised the stick again.

"Andrew, drop the stick," Damen yelled, rushing forward. Billy, arms up, stared at Andrew, Ricky, and Damen, all poised to fight.

Damen reached for the stick. "Andrew!" he shouted again, but Andrew swung it over his head and in front of their faces. Billy rolled away to avoid being hit.

"Try *me*, you coward," screamed Ricky, his fists clenched.

"Back off. Back off, all of you," Andrew yelled as he jabbed the stick at Ricky. His lips quivered, and he taunted the crowd, jumping and waving the stick around like a crazed ninja. Everyone scurried out of Andrew's way. Keeping his eyes fixed on Andrew, Billy rose to his feet.

"I'm going to get a supervisor," someone from the crowd said.

Voices from the crowd boiled over, attacking Andrew. "You're out of your tree. Crazy. You've lost it, man."

Billy reached to help Amy, but before he could pull her up, Andrew's foot lashed out and caught him in the groin. He groaned and doubled over in pain. Andrew caught him in a headlock and jammed the stick into his gut. Despite the sharp pain and a sudden numbing cold around him, Billy swept his leg to knock Andrew down. As he fell, Andrew growled, smacking Billy in the head with the stick and kneeing him in the stomach. Vomit seared Billy's throat, and his gut cramped. Choking it back down, he slammed his fist into Andrew's jaw. The crowd shouted as he struggled to keep Andrew from ripping him apart.

An arm pulled on Billy's leg, freeing him from Andrew's grip. Damen grappled with Andrew's arm, and Ricky tried to hold his legs. Billy snatched at an arm, but it was like trying to grab an octopus. The stick flew from Andrew's grip, parting his hair as it whizzed by. He wrestled with the arm, but Andrew's limbs flailed, tripping him. Falling, his elbow slammed into An- drew's nose and blood sprayed everywhere. Andrew howled, shook them off, and drove his knee into Billy's middle again while clawing at his eyes like a mad crow. Hot bile scorched his throat, and he puked on his attacker. Ricky and Damen jumped back. Kids groaned and laughed, shuffling out of the way, some gagging and others cheering.

Billy wiped his mouth with his hand and choked more bile down, his face flushed and his head throbbing. Andrew shoved him away and sprang to his feet, tore his smelly jacket off, and wiped his bloody face with his sleeve. "Thanks a lot, puke boy," he said. His hands shook as he leaned over Billy, wiping the vomit from his pants.

"Totally awesome, man!" someone yelled.

"What is going on?" a supervisor's voice yelled from across the field.

Blood pounded in Billy's head. He coughed and choked, his stomach churning. He rolled on the grass, spitting vomit from his

13

mouth. Finally, he sucked in a deep breath and lay exhausted on the grass. His senses cleared, he rose to his knees and looked around. Ricky and Damen faced Andrew, ready for round two. Billy took in the torn shirts, mud-covered pants, vomit, blood and grass stains and prayed it was over.

Andrew, nose still dripping blood, wiped his sleeve over his face and staggered. He shook his head. "What are you staring at?" he snarled at Ricky as the supervisors approached.

"A bloody mess," Ricky said, shoving Andrew away.

Here we go again.

Andrew pounced on Ricky, who jumped to his right and stuck his leg out. Andrew caught Ricky's coat on the way down, and they tumbled together onto the grass.

"Boys. Boys. Break it up, you two. The rest of you come on, the show's over, back to your games." Two playground supervisors pulled Andrew and Ricky apart. Andrew's nose poured blood again, soaking his shirt and Ms. Thompson's hands. She mopped up the gore with several tissues she pulled from her pocket. Billy stared at the smelly mess and smiled in spite of his aching head and sore stomach. *Serves him right.*

"What do you think you're doing?" Mrs. Cleghorne demanded, her hands on her hips. Billy held his gut and groaned while Ms. Thompson pinched Andrew's nose and tilted his head back. Ricky and Damen cleaned the mud from their clothes, but none of them said anything.

Mrs. Cleghorne faced the remaining crowd. "There's nothing more to see," she said. They muttered and scattered across the field.

"What's going to happen to them?" one of Andrew's friends asked.

"That's not your concern. Run along now," said Ms. Thompson, letting go of Andrew's nose.

"What happened here?" Mrs. Cleghorne asked.

Becky Ronson, who was helping Amy clean up, piped in. "They were fighting because Andrew bullied Amy."

"Amy, what were they doing?"

"W-well, ma'am," Amy said. "A-Andrew and D- Damen called me names, and A-Andrew hit me with a stick."

Becky, her usual busybody self, added, "Then Ricky and Billy came to help her, and Andrew started fighting and—"

"Thank you, Becky. Boys, head to the office right now," Mrs. Cleghorne ordered. Billy tucked his grass-stained shirt into his pants, ran his sleeve across his mouth, and brushed the mud off his clothes. The boys shuffled behind Mrs. Thompson. Billy took in the bruised and muddy faces, scratched arms, and torn clothing. *We look like a beaten-up army troop.* He wrinkled his nose, realizing he smelled like a walking bowl of barf. Glancing back, he met Andrew's eyes for a second. They glowed and blinked again. Billy shivered as a dark presence touched him. Andrew's eyes cleared, and a look of terror flitted across his face. *What was that?* Andrew looked lost and confused and then shook himself and sneered at Billy.

"Smooth move, ex-lax," Andrew said at the door.

"Shut up, Andrew," Billy replied. "You shouldn't have hit Amy with the stick."

"What...what stick? What are you talking about?" Andrew's jaw dropped.

"Oh, come on, Andrew." Ricky raised his eye- brows.

"You started it, Billy," Andrew said. "I was only teasing."

"Yeah, right," Ricky added, rolling his eyes. "How do you tease with a stick?"

Andrew opened his mouth, but Mrs. Thompson broke in, "Boys, not one more word! You can tell it to the principal!" She flung open the door. An icy chill crawled down Billy's spine. *What was in Andrew's eyes?*

— CHAPTER THREE —

Amy

At the office, Mrs. Cleghorne pointed to the chairs. "Sit down and wait for the principal." She separated the boys—Billy and Ricky under the window, Damen over by the medical room—before she stalked out. Andrew, his nose bleeding again, scowled at Ricky and Billy as he shuffled off to the washroom.

Talking her ear off, Becky led a tearful Amy into the office. "Don't pay any attention to those mean boys; they don't know what they're talking about. I think you look real nice and—"

"Are you okay?" the secretary asked, handing Amy a Kleenex.

"The boys were teasing her, and Andrew tore her blouse and hit her on the head with a stick," Becky said. Amy wiped tears from her eyes.

"Oh, my goodness," the secretary said when she touched Amy's head. "You've got quite a lump there. Let's get some ice on that." She draped her arm around Amy and walked her into the medical room. Becky pushed her black-rimmed glasses up her nose and stuck her tongue out at Damen when she brushed by him. He laughed and muttered something Billy didn't catch.

"She's such a busybody," Ricky whispered.

"Yeah, always yapping about something. I wonder if she talks in her sleep, too," Billy said.

Ricky snickered. "No wonder she doesn't have any friends," he said.

Billy giggled. He lowered his aching head onto his arms and closed his eyes. *What a stupid start to grade seven. I'll probably be suspended, and Dad will ground me for a week. It's not fair; I was only trying to help Amy.*

Andrew returned from the washroom, a cloth on the back of his neck. Pinching his nose, he flopped down in a chair beside Damen. *Andrew seems so different. He's never hit anyone with a stick before. Those eyes...* Ricky nudged Billy, and he popped his head up.

Ms. Fenton bustled in, her arms full of papers. "Donna, I need you to phone Mr. Jackson for me and make an appointment for next week—where is she?"

"I'll be right there," the secretary called from the medical room. Billy cringed when the principal focused her stern gaze on them.

"You're the boys who were fighting on the playground? The first day of school?"Billy chewed his lip. *Oh boy, now I'm in for it.*

Ricky looked up from a book he held in his hands. Damen slumped lower in his perch, and Andrew sighed heavily.

Ms. Fenton's heels clicked as she walked to her office. She turned and pointed her finger at Billy and Ricky. "You two, come in and tell me what happened."She held the door for them. Andrew snorted when they walked past, and the principal shut the door firmly. She pulled a pen and notepad from her desk caddie. "Billy, why don't you start?"

"Well, Andrew and Damen were teasing Amy," Billy said, nervously rubbing his hands. The boys told her what had happened, and Ms. Fenton took notes. Billy's face burned every time she raised her eyebrows or cleared her throat. She tapped her pen on the desk, and he squirmed in his chair. He didn't tell her about Andrew being different or about how his voice changed to that harsh, deep rasp and the yellow glow of his eyes. Just thinking about it made his heart pound and his palms slick.

"Thank you, boys," she said at last. "You can go back out and wait in the office. Andrew, come in, please." Andrew, his face a white sheet, sighed when he passed them.

When they sat down on the bench, Ricky whispered, "I think he's in for it."

"He deserves it. He should be suspended." "I hope we don't get suspended, too."

"We only tried to help," Billy said, not sure who he was trying to convince, his friend or himself. He saw those yellow eyes staring at him again. *He was acting weird.*

17

"What do you mean you don't know what happened?" the principal's voice pierced through his thoughts. "You started a fight and struck two people with a stick!"

Billy rubbed the lump on his head. *And I've got the headache to prove it.* The boys were startled when the secretary pushed herself out of her chair with a screech and went into the medical room.

Ms. Fenton continued her tirade. "Fighting is not allowed at school!" *Too late for that.*

The secretary returned to her desk. "Did either of you see Amy leave?" she asked. The boys shook their heads. She picked up the phone and called around—Mr. Moore, the supervisors, and the janitor—but no one had seen Amy since she'd entered the medical room.

"You are one of the seniors this year. You should know better!" Ms. Fenton yelled. *Usually, he's too smart to do something dumb like this.* Billy sighed and rubbed his face. *I guess I should know better, too.*

"Hitting people with a stick—that's assault!" Billy could see the principal through the window in the door; she was on her feet, her hands flailing like an angry blackbird, her voice squawking as she tore a strip off Andrew. Billy shuddered. *What about the crows on the roof and their weird dance and chatter? That man with the stick in the window.*

"I can't wait for our turn," he whispered to Ricky. "Remember, we tried to protect her."

"Yeah, but I was fighting."

"You mean defending yourself. Andrew started it." "But I continued it." Billy rubbed his hands.

"You were sticking up for Amy. Nobody else was, right?"

"This behavior is intolerable! Do you understand me?" The principal yelled and sat back down. Billy jumped and rubbed his face. *He'll be lucky if he isn't sus- pended for a month. And what about me?*

The walkie-talkie clicked. "We've checked all over the school, even the kiln room, and there's no sign of Amy," a voice said.

I'm not surprised she's missing; after everything that happened today—the face in the window, the wind, Andrew's weird behavior—what next?

"Better check outside," the secretary said. She dropped the walkie-talkie, bustled over to the principal's office and knocked on the door.

"Come in," Ms. Fenton barked.

"Amy is gone," the secretary said as she pushed the door open.

"What do you mean; *she's gone?*" the principal asked.

"We can't find her."

"What?" Ms. Fenton scowled.

"She's not in the medical room, and we've checked the whole school." The secretary sounded flustered.

Ms. Fenton rose from her desk. "Andrew, go back to class. Donna, call her room again." The secretary dashed back to her desk. Andrew grunted when he passed Ricky and Billy on his way out of the office. *Maybe Andrew dodged a bullet.*

Ms. Fenton eyed the boys. "Go back to class, you three. We'll finish this later." Damen rose and followed Andrew. The principal stood in the doorway and tapped her nails on the doorframe. "She has to be here somewhere, Donna."

Not necessarily. Have you tried the attic or the bell tower? Maybe ask the crows.

When they reached the library, Billy gasped. A blond ponytail and a green skirt just like Amy's disappeared around the corner of the upstairs landing. He grabbed Ricky's arm. "Look. There she is," he whispered, pointing up the stairs.

"Come on, Billy, I don't see anything. This whole thing has got you spooked." Ricky pulled his arm free.

"No, she was there. I'm sure. Let's go check."

They ran up the stairs and searched the hall. "I don't see anything," Ricky said.

"Over by the tower," Billy said. "I have a funny feeling she's there." By the gym doors, they looked up through the glass floor of the bell tower. Light from the outside glinted down, mixed with shadows where the bell hung inside the small room.

Ricky raised his hands. "There's nothing here."

A grey form flew across the glass and disappeared. "Whoa. Did you see that?" Billy asked, a twinge creep- ing down his spine.

"I sure did." Ricky grabbed Billy's arm. Their eyes met, and Billy felt him shiver.

"What *was* that?" Billy croaked, craning his neck to see more. They stood there like trapped mice waiting for a cat.

"Maybe we should get out of here." Ricky turned away.

"What are you boys doing?" demanded Ms. Overon. The boys jumped at her voice and turned around, guilt all over their faces.

"Ah, we were going to the washroom," Billy said, letting go of Ricky and gulping down his fear, "when we saw something up in the tower."

The librarian raised her eyebrows. "Really? What did you see?"

"It was like a shadow moving across the glass," Ricky said.

"More like a ghost," Billy muttered.

"A ghost? Probably just sun and shadow from above," Ms. Overon said. "Anyway, head back to class. It's just about time to go home."

"Yes, ma'am," Billy answered, pulling Ricky down the hall.

The Crows

The next morning, the school grounds were empty, and the sun warmed Billy as he watched the birds chirping and gliding over the field. He relaxed into the quiet morning peace and leaned against the warm bricks. No crows were in sight on the roof or in the oak trees. *It is going to be a better day, today.*

Ricky entered the gates and ran up to join him. A crow scolded from the roof as Ricky tossed his backpack beside Billy's. Several other crows collected along the gutter, squawking like a demented choir. Billy nervously eyed the tower above—would the face appear again?

"Are you looking for that ghost again?" Ricky asked.

Billy started. His friend had just about read his mind, but he answered calmly, "No, just watching the crows."

"Do you think Amy is a ghost?"

He frowned. "No, I thought I saw her yesterday, but that grey thing in the tower, *that* was something else."

"Maybe it's that old guy you saw at the window." Ricky turned his head and squinted at the roof. The tack, tack, tack of the crows' talons beat in time with the caws and squawks as the birds danced, shaking their wings and pecking at each other. More circled and joined in the cacophony until they covered the roof in black, feathered shapes.

"Look at all the crows," Billy said. The black mass cawed, lifted off the roof and spiraled down toward them. "Ricky, get off the stairs," he shouted. Grabbing his friend by the arm, he bounded down with the murder of crows jabbing and scratching at them.

"Cover your face." Billy swatted at the black mass of wings, beaks, and claws. Panicked, the boys dove into the hollow under the stone steps. Ricky crouched on the cement with his coat pulled over his head. An enormous crow pecked at the back of his neck and dug into his back.

"Get it off, get it off !" Ricky's voice trembled and broke.

21

"Get off him!" Billy screeched, flapping his arms at it. The black terror spread its wings, cawing and flailing at him. He stared into its alien, yellow eyes. A cold chill ran through his bones as he smacked at it. The bird cawed like a raven and lunged at him, its wings whipping into his face. When the oily feathers smacked his mouth, it tasted like a birdbath, and its foul breath reeked. He swatted at it in desperation. The black birds lashed his cheek, drawing blood. Billy howled and swiped at it again. He missed, and it flew up and out of the hollow, joining the black mass outside.

He drew in a deep shaking breath as he wiped the blood on his sleeve and sat back on the cement. The cawing, rustling noises of the birds ended like some magical force had silenced them. The heavy stillness weighed on him, and his head reeled, adrenaline still pumping. He caught his breath, taking in Ricky crouched over and shivering while he waited for the world to rotate again.

"You okay?" He shook his friend, his heart thumping.

"Yes, I think so." Ricky sat up. "What the hell was that? Those birds, the noise."

"I-I don't know, but that was *not* normal." He hugged his friend and tried to pull himself together, trying to grab onto some reason, but none came. Billy caught his breath and peered out at the school grounds. Everything looked peaceful again; birds chirped and flew through the trees, sunlight glanced off the cement, while kids ran, laughed, and yelled all over the schoolyard—no crows, no yellow eyes, no ghosts. *Did that really happen?*

"It's all clear," Billy said, dazed but relieved. Ricky peeked out before they crawled from their hiding place. Kids stood by the stairs, teasing each other and playing. *Didn't they see the birds?* The boys climbed the stairs and peered up at the roof. The black birds clung to the gutter and stared back in silence. Gingerly, Billy picked up his backpack. "Ricky, let's go to the playground. I don't trust those crows," he whispered.

"Me neither." They flew down the stairs and swung around the corner of the brick wall, running straight into Andrew and Damen. All four boys spilled onto the cement.

"S-sorry," Billy said as they stood up.

"What's your problem, puke boy? A ghost chasing you?" Andrew said, frowning.

"Never mind, Andrew," Billy said, trying to pass him.

Andrew sneered and grabbed Billy's arm. "*Never mind?* You got me in trouble, Billy boy," Andrew said. "I got a week's in-school suspension, thanks to you. And you got nothing."

"Back off," Ricky said, pushing Andrew's arm away and bumping Damen.

"Oooo, I'm scared," Damen said as he waved his arms and stepped in front of Ricky."Maybe you should join that Amy kid in the tower, Ricky. You'd fit right in with those hand-me-down clothes you wear."

"You too, Billy; after all, she's your girlfriend," Andrew said, stepping in front of him again.

"Shut up!" Ricky dropped his backpack and grabbed Damen's arm.

Damen stepped back, shaking him loose and chuckled. "Ooo-la-la," he said as he swung his backpack around.

"Yeah, Ricky you—"

Michael Davidson strode around the corner, slurped on a can of soda, and burped. "Hey, guys, you want to play soccer out back?"

"Sure, Mike," Billy said, reaching down and grabbing his backpack.

Andrew grabbed Billy's arm again. "Nah, Mike, Billy and I have a score to settle—right, Billy?"

"Forget it." He shook himself free. "I'm not getting in any more trouble because of you."

"*More* trouble. You didn't get in *any* trouble, you chicken."

"Chicken," Damen said. He clucked and waved his arms.

"Come on, let's go." Billy ignored them and grabbed Ricky's arm. They ran to catch up with Mike.

Several minutes later, the school buzzer rang, and everyone headed to his or her line-ups. On the way in, Ricky pointed to a window upstairs in the gymnasium. "Look up there," he said. Billy followed his gaze and saw a girl's face. Her hair shone in the sunlight. He dropped his pack and squinted. Using his hand to shield his eyes from the glare, he watched her wave at them.

"Did you see that?" Billy asked. He couldn't believe what he saw.

"Yeah, and you know who she looks like?"

"Amy." Billy picked his pack up. "Maybe a ghost *is* after us."

"Boys, what are you two lollygagging about?" Mrs. Smithson, one of the supervisors, asked, her arms crossed.

"Ah, nothing," Billy answered. The boys trudged over to the line-up. When the kids entered, Ms. Fenton greeted them.

"Ms. Fenton?" Ricky asked. "Yes, Ricky?"

"Did you find that missing girl? Amy Sutherland?"

"Don't worry about her. It's all taken care of," the principal said. Billy caught Ricky's eyes and winked. *Is it really taken care of?* Hanging up his backpack, he looked around for Amy, who wasn't there. *Maybe she just shows up when she feels like it, like those latchkey kids who don't seem to have parents.* He took his seat. *Maybe she comes and goes as she pleases because she is a ghost. Does that figure in the tower have something to do with Amy's disappearance? And Andrew's behavior still doesn't make sense. Not to mention those crows—are they possessed or something?*

CHAPTER FIVE

The Library

"She stepped up into the old red truck as her father cranked the ignition, threw it into first gear, and drove down the dirt driveway, kicking up dust behind them. This would be her first trip to town, and it felt good to be able to travel with her father. He usually went alone or with her mother, but Mother was ill and said Grace could go along in her place. She would get to see all the shops and the city girls and maybe even get some candy at Mr. Morgan's Confectionary. The nickels that Mother had given her for her tenth birthday jangled in her old purse, which had also been a tenth birthday gift from her mother, as she imagined herself a rich young lady coming from her country estate to do business in the city. As they drove away, her father turned on the radio, and one of his favorite songs was playing. They sang it together as he drove through the gate."

Ms. Overon, the librarian, read from the book they had been listening to for a few weeks now. It was about a girl growing up in the fifties. Billy's grandmother told him they played in a wood called *'the transfer'* back then. It was a stretch of forest between the school and Grandma's house. She called it her "idyllic playground of childhood," where you could climb tall trees, pick violets and Easter lilies while playing hide-n-seek. She told him her stories of how they were afraid to walk the trails. The thick forest was dark and scary, with the wind whistling and the black birds diving at them on their way to school. Her tales of the Boogie Man lurking behind a tree reminded him of the face in the window, and he shivered.

The librarian glanced at her watch. "It's time to find a book," she said. "You have about ten minutes to browse and read. Then you have to choose one of the books to checkout." All of the kids headed to the shelves and the stacks of books. Billy pulled several books from the shelves. *The Emily Carr Mystery* sounded cool until he read about it being a love story. He put it back and pulled out "The Saxe Point Park Mystery." *This is more like it, a story about a park I play in, and it has magical objects and stuff. Cool.* He set it aside and grabbed another title that caught his eye, "A Perfect Gentle Knight." *Knights of the Round Table and Sir Lancelot—this is the one.* He made his way over to where Ricky sat, thumbing through what looked like an old history book. He sat down beside his friend and started reading.

"Look at this." Ricky held the old book under Billy's nose.

Billy frowned at his friend. "I'm reading," he said.

"Just look for a second." Ricky strained to hold the heavy book up.

"All right." He put his book down and gazed at a class photo of kids. "What is it?"

"A History of Esquimalt."

"So?"

"So, this is Lampson Street School, *our* school."

"Yeah? Let me see. The kids are dressed funny, aren't they? I wonder if my grandpa's picture is in here. Let me see." He grabbed the book, and they thumbed through the pages together.

"Hey, stop." Ricky grabbed Billy's hand as he turned the pages. "Go back, go back."

"There, there." He tapped his finger on a picture of a group of adults. "Look at that guy. He's bald on top, and he's wearing a bowtie." They both laughed.

Billy read the caption. "His name is Mr. Olsen. He was one of the teachers. And look at the guy beside him. It says: *Mr. Maynard. Max, the ghost that haunts the bell tower!*"

"He must have been a teacher back then. No wonder he's a ghost." They laughed again.

Billy pointed to the bottom of the page. "Look at this picture." A boys' basketball team stood proud and tall, the captain accepting the winner's cup from a school official's hand. However, the paintings on the walls behind the team caught his attention with pictures of eagles, whales, and salmon.

Ricky leaned forward to get a better look. "That's First Nations' artwork," he said.

"Is that a whale?"

"Could be, and that looks like a totem."

Billy pointed to a stylized bird just above a bald man's head. "Hey, look, there's a raven. He's cool." The raven looked like he was about to land on the shiny, rounded dome.

"I wouldn't want to be that guy, eh?" Ricky said.

The boys laughed.

"That's the gym upstairs. I wonder what happened to the pictures?"

"Good question, man."

"Look at what the kids are wearing in this picture." "Yeah, pretty lame if you ask me. The girls have long dresses with bows in the front, and the boys are wearing short pants, long socks, and bowties—yuck."

"Yeah, you wouldn't catch me dead in that stuff. It must be the Fall Festival. Look at all the parents in the photo."

"And the size of that pumpkin. No wonder there's a big purple ribbon on it."

"And look, they're having an egg and spoon race. You can see that girl dropped her egg on the floor; only the picture must have caught it just before it landed.

Billy jammed his finger into his friend's arm. "Look at that boy holding the big ribbon."

"Yeah, so?" Ricky rubbed his arm.

"That's my grandpa."

"For real?"

"Shhh!" Two girls sitting beside them at the library table warned. Billy made a face at them.

"I think he's presenting it to a teacher. Isn't that cool? Imagine, my grand—"

"Hold on, look at the girl in this picture," Ricky whispered. He pointed at a light-haired girl with a big smile on the opposite page. She wore a light, flowered dress under a white smock. "Who does she remind you of?"

Billy leaned over and squinted. "Amy? Amy Sutherland?"

"It sure looks like her, doesn't it?"

"Uh huh, must be her grandmother or something.

I wonder if she knew my grandpa."

"Yeah, maybe. Look at the date, April 10, 1955." "I'm going to take out this book. I want to try and figure out who she is."

"Maybe she just looks like her." "Maybe she's a ghost." They laughed.

"Who's a ghost?" Becky asked as she carried an armful of books to check out.

"Nobody, Becky." Billy closed the book and rolled his eyes. "I was reading a scary story about a ghost."

"You sure read weird stuff," she said, craning her neck to try to read the title. Billy shoved the book under his arm.

"Why don't you mind your own business?" Ricky said.

"Humph." Becky pushed her glasses up her nose and dropped her books on the counter. "You should try reading something good like *The Babysitters Club*." The boys snickered.

Back in class, Billy opened up the book and flipped through the pages until he found the picture again. He ran his finger over the students' photos until he reached the girl who looked like Amy. There was a phenomenal resemblance, the same hair, dress, and smile. *It's just a coincidence.* Her face did look a little thinner, and her hair was done up in a bun.

"Hello, Amy," Mr. Moore said. Billy looked up.

"Sorry I'm late, sir, but I had an appointment this morning." Billy's head bobbed up and down as he stared back and forth, comparing Amy's hair, eyes, and clothes to the photo.

"Better late than never," the teacher said. "Take your seat, please." Amy nodded, smiled at Billy, and sat at her desk. He studied her clothes closely. Her skirt had red and green flowers on it. He scanned the photo. *Of course, the dress is actually a skirt and blouse. Amy is just wearing a different blouse today—a white one that doesn't match the skirt.*

Billy stiffened. He looked up at Amy, facing the front. All he could see was part of her forehead and cheek, but that was enough. He stared at the photo, squinting hard to make it out. He brushed his hand over the page, but it was not a fleck of eraser, or a piece of dust. He focused on her cheek, then the photo, before falling back in his seat. They both had the exact same scar on their cheeks. Amy was not this girl's granddaughter. Amy *was* this girl.

— CHAPTER SIX —

Andrew

Billy looked at the triangle in front of him and scratched his head. Finding the area of a triangle was different from finding the area of a square. Just like Amy was different. If she was from the past, why was she here? He looked at her, but no answer came back. *How does she travel through time? I know; she takes triangles and builds them into polygons of time.* Oh, brother, I'm getting nowhere. He shook his head, put his pencil down, and eyed the clock on the wall. *Ah, recess.*

The bell rang, and the kids swarmed out. Billy looked for Ricky by the door, noticed he was still at his desk, and hurried back to him.

"Come on, man." Billy danced around the desk, tapped his fingers, and tore the pencil from his hand. "I want to ask Amy about those photos in that book. Hurry up, she's already left."

"Take it easy, man. I'm coming. I just had to write down that last question for homework." When Ricky rose, Billy grabbed his books, shoved them into the desk, and pulled him toward the door. "I'm coming, I'm coming," he said, pulling his arm back.

"Just a minute, boys," Mr. Moore said at the door. The janitor stood beside him with his garbage cart. "Mr. Armstrong needs some help at recess. Would you boys be willing to give him a hand?"

"Well, I-I..." Billy said, raising his hand and looking over at Ricky.

"Pardon me?" Mr. Moore asked, his hand on Billy's shoulder.

"I guess so, sir." Billy looked at his feet.

"Good," said Mr. Armstrong. The boys followed him into the hall. They emptied garbage cans, wiped chalk dust rails, and collected dirty brushes from the classrooms. Billy kept glancing at his watch as he worked. Several times, he dropped brushes or spilt the garbage in his haste.

Entering the detention room, he gulped. Andrew sat at a table in the middle of the room and scribbled on some paper. A little kid colored beside him.

"What are you doing in here, puke boy?" Andrew asked. He crossed his arms and slumped in his chair. "Got a detention, too, eh?"

"No, we're just helping the janitor." Billy picked up the trashcan.

Andrew pointed his pencil at Billy. "I'm not finished with you, loser. You know that, right?"

"Forget it, Andrew. It's over." Billy squinted at the drawing. Under the picture, it read, *Puke boy will get his*. His cheeks burned, but he shook it off.

"Over? It didn't even start for *you!*" Andrew's chair screeched as he pushed it away from the table. The little kid's eyes bulged, and his mouth gaped like a fish. He jumped up, dropped his crayon, and flew over to the couch in the corner.

"I got in trouble at home," Billy said.

"Sure you did!" Andrew crumpled up his picture and hurled it at Billy, who dropped the garbage can and ducked.

Ricky whipped around to face Andrew. "Give it a break, Andrew. You know why you got into trouble."

"Who asked you, Rick, the dick?" Andrew said. "You think you're always right just because your dad's a dick, too?"

Ricky slapped the cleaning cloth against the chalk rail. "At least *my* dad cares about me." Andrew looked stunned for a second but covered it, except for the glint of tears in his eyes. "Yeah, right," he said. "That's why he's never home? Because he spends so much time with you?"

Ricky's shoulders hunched as the taunt hit home. He stepped toward Andrew, his fists clenched.

"Come on, Ricky. We're finished here."Billy turned and headed out of the room.

"Right," Ricky said. He stared Andrew down on his way out.

"I'll see you two after school," he called after them. In the hallway, Billy pushed the cart to the next room. "You got him choked. What did you mean about his father?"

Ricky gathered up the brushes. "You know when we change for gym class?"

"Yeah." Billy emptied the wastebasket.

Ricky dropped the brushes into the cleaning box, darting a glance at his friend and back. "Have you ever looked at Andrew's back and legs?"

"No, not really. Why would I?"

"He's got bruises on them."

"I guess he does, but he says he's always falling be- cause he's clumsy."

Ricky stared at Billy, his eyebrows raised. "Have you ever seen him trip or fall on the soccer field?"

"Not any more than anyone else."

"And how about in gym?" They pushed the cart down the hall.

"Nope. Come to think of it, he's pretty good at sports." Billy stopped, his eyes widening. "Oh!"

Ricky leaned over the cart, glanced up and down the hallway, and whispered, "My dad has been called to his house a few times. Last week they took Andrew's dad to the police station."

Billy nodded. "No wonder he acts like such a smart-ass."

Ricky pushed the cart. "It all makes sense, doesn't it?" he said as they passed the library.

"It sure does." Billy spied the janitor coming up the stairs.

"Ah, boys. Thank you so much for doing those rooms. It's a big help."

"No problem, Mr. Armstrong," Billy said. He looked at his watch. "Come on, Ricky. We've got a few minutes left." They headed outside, and the buzzer blared from the speaker above them.

"Rats! We'll have to catch her at lunch."

"At least we're first at the fountain," Ricky said, pumping water into his mouth.

CHAPTER SEVEN

The Ocular Orb

Back in class, Billy tapped his fingers on his desk in frustration. He sent thoughts to the back of Amy's head just before Mr. Moore started his lessons. *Where are you from, and why are you here? How can I talk to you before lunch? Maybe I can pull the fire alarm? No, bad idea. Maybe the secretary will call you to the office. Or not.* He picked up his pencil and chewed on the end. *If I have to wait until lunch, you might disappear again. Maybe we will have an earthquake. Fat chance of that. Maybe I'm just dreaming, and I'll wake up in my bed.* Billy sighed and chewed his pencil again as Mr. Moore droned on.

Partway through spelling, Amy raised her hand and asked to go to the washroom. *Yes.* Billy raised his hand. Mr. Moore gave permission, and Billy winked at Ricky, their signal for "meet me in the washroom," before he dashed from the room.

From the main floor, Billy heard Amy's footsteps on the stairs. He bounded up after her. On the second floor, he heard the gym door bang shut. He darted to the doors, looked through the glass, and watched her take a round, shiny object from her pocket. A bright light flashed, and the stage wavered as if it were under water. "Whoa, what's that?" he said as he opened the door.

Amy muttered some strange words, and a loud, whirring sound struck his ears. A strong wind snatched the door from his hand and slammed it against the wall. Billy grabbed the doorframe with one hand, the other shielding his eyes as he peered through the swirling torrent of dust. The blinds rattled, and wall posters flew in every direction like demented kites. Soccer balls rolled, and colored team jerseys flew like butterflies about the room.

Billy's grip gave way as the air sucked him forward like a giant vacuum. He rolled across the floor and yelped in pain when his shoulder slammed into a bench. In desperation, he grabbed a piano leg to anchor himself.

He shivered in a heap, his heart thumping, hands shaking. The gym looked like a carnival in a tornado. On the stage, a table lay upside down, and a chair on top of it was draped with torn colored jerseys. The stage curtains swirled like dancers, and the backlights flashed on and off in greens and reds. Soccer balls bounced off the walls as if ghosts were playing a game. The howling vortex whipped all around him. He clung to the piano leg while praying for the turmoil to subside.

Without warning, the wind died. The lights stopped flashing; the balls stopped bouncing. He slid from under the piano and watched a poster float back to earth. The stage curtains rocked back and forth, but the mess was gone, and only the blinds hung askew in some strange new geometry. A magical janitor must have cleaned it up in seconds. Billy stared at the stage. "Amy? Where did you go?"

"Was she here?" Ricky asked.

"Ah!" Billy started and whirled around.

Ricky paced across the gym toward him. "Are you okay?"

"I think so." Billy rubbed his shoulder and leaned against the stage.

"What happened?"

"I'm not sure. One minute she was here; the next, she was gone!"

"Amy? What do you mean, *gone*?"

Billy stared at his friend. "She held this round thing in her hand, spoke some strange words, and a tornado sprung up and blew everything all over."

Ricky raised an eyebrow and looked around the gym— quiet, neat, and tidy. "A tornado? You're kidding, right?"

"It happened so fast. By the time I caught my breath, she was gone."

"Are you sure she disappeared? She didn't just sneak out while you weren't looking?"

"Sure as I'm standing here." Billy looked at the spotless floor. He shuddered, half expecting something to jump out at him.

Ricky hopped up on the stage. "You sure you're all right? You don't look so good."

Billy winced, rubbed his shoulder, and boosted himself up beside his friend. He felt like he had lost a battle with a grizzly. "I'm okay. Just a little shook up." The gym was as quiet as a tomb. *It's too still.* The only sound he heard was a light tap as the blinds slapped against the sill. *Go back, go back, go back,* they seemed to say. Billy grabbed the edge of the stage as it rolled under him like a boat in the ocean.

"Whoa!" he said. "Did you feel that?"

"I sure did! What's going on?" Ricky jumped off the stage and eyed it suspiciously.

Billy hopped down, too. "I think it's going to happen again!"They crept away as the stage wavered like a bowl of jelly.

"I don't like this." Ricky grabbed Billy's arm.

Go back, go back, go back, the blinds warned. The boys huddled together, their eyes fixed on the stage. The curtains swayed, the floor rolled, and a cold gust of wind pulled at their hair and clothes. Billy shivered as the temperature plummeted.

"What's doing that?" Ricky asked.

"Hold on!" Billy yelled, steadying himself.

"Agh!" Ricky shrieked; the wind howled, yanking them horizontally and flinging them onto the floor.

"Ow!" Billy shouted as Ricky's knee caught him in the head where he lay on his back. The posters, jer- seys, and soccer balls flew in every direction. The wind sucked them both across the floor and pinned them against the stage. One of the balls flew by their heads and out an open window. Billy reached up and grabbed the handle of a storage cupboard.

"It will stop in a minute," Billy said. The door slammed shut, the whirring wind stopped abruptly, and the boys panted like dogs on the floor. The balls bounced over them, and jerseys draped their heads. They threw them off and stood on the stage; the curtains swayed, and Amy appeared. "W-where did you come from?" he asked.

"And where is the mess?" Ricky asked, surveying the tidy gym.

"From the past. It's time for you to come, too. Here, take my hand." She pulled a spherical object from her pocket. "Ricky, grab Billy's hand."

Ricky stepped back. "I don't know about this," he said.

"Amy, what are you doing?"Billy asked.

"You'll see," she said as she held the shiny object in front of her. Billy reached over and grabbed Ricky's hand. "*Oculus me ad praeteritum.*" The wind pulled on them again. Billy squeezed Amy's hand and took a deep breath.

"What the—" Ricky started. Billy heard him wheeze, but the torrent of air took away his voice and yanked them into blackness.

Billy lost his bearings, and they catapulted through the ether. His heart pounded. He held his breath because the nothingness had no substance. He spiraled through the void like an iron filing pulled toward a magnet. Spots danced before his eyes; he heard nothing, saw nothing—the only sensation was the warmth of Amy's fingers.

His ears popped. Light and colors burst in front of his eyes. The air hit him like a tonic. He filled his lungs like a baby's first breath, savoring the moment, and felt blood rush through his arms and legs. His feet struck a wood floor, spilling him over it. Amy, still holding his hand, tumbled head over heels. The walls spun around him; he smelled musty paint and waited for the vertigo to stop. Amy let go. She rose to her feet and shook her head. Ricky's form, grey in the semi-dark, swam in front of Billy's eyes for a moment and then steadied.

It was the gym, all right, but it was not *his* gym. The floor was old and dusty, with rectangles of light from the sunlight that filtered around the edges of the dark blinds, shining on the gym floor. It was different from the slatted bands that the Venetian blinds made. Painted pictures covered the walls. Where was he? Or maybe he should ask, *when* was he?

Amy leaned against a pillar. She reached up and flicked a switch. Light from round overhead globes pierced the gloom. They were not the fluorescents of his gym.

"Amy, where are we?" Ricky asked, rubbing his head.

"Welcome to the fifties. Pretty cool, eh?" Amy said, pirouetting around a pillar.

Billy surveyed the room. The walls, covered in murals, depicted First Nations' life before the Europeans. Even the pillars, spaced around the room, looked like totem poles of wolves, bears, and eagles—complete with wings—and climbed the columns toward a huge raven perched in a fir tree, stern eyes overlooking the village. "Those are the murals we saw in the library book, Ricky."

"Yeah! They're awesome!" Ricky walked toward a giant black and white orca swimming alongside a canoe filled with First Nations people.

"Look at the stage," Billy said. A long house, complete with rising smoke, stood above the wooden surface with painted totems erected on either side. Ravens and eagles watched over the beach where cedar logs and canoes rested. "The canoes smell like real cedar."

"And the totems have been carved," Ricky said. "All we need now are real people."

"This is cool, Amy, but why did you bring us here?" Billy asked.

"And can we get back?" Ricky added.

"Of course, we can. We just traveled through time, that's all."

"That's all! *Just* traveled through time. Sure, Amy, I travel to Saturn every Tuesday in a UFO. No problem." Billy rolled his eyes.

"How is this possible?" Ricky asked.

"Shhh. Someone is coming," Amy said, pointing to the gym door, which creaked open. A tall man in dark clothes stepped in. He stopped a few feet from them and thumped a black cane on the floor like a drill sergeant. Billy stared, his heartbeat rising. A tingle ran down his spine: *A man with a cane.*

37

The man tapped the cane against his foot. "What are you children doing up here?" His boney fingers played like a spider over the white knob. No one spoke.

The man frowned at them and rapped the cane once more. "Well? I asked you what you are doing up here?" His brow creased, and he pointed the cane at the children. Billy shivered and looked back at Amy.

"We're getting ready for the concert, sir," she said. "We have to go downstairs now." She pulled Billy toward a door at the back of the gym. Ricky followed.

"Come back here!" the man yelled. "I'm not finished with you." The cane thudded on the floor as he spoke.

"Hurry," Amy said. She yanked them out into the hall and down the stairs.

"Who is that creepy guy?" Billy asked.

"He sure is a miserable dude," Ricky said when they had reached the main floor.

"That 'miserable dude' is Mr. Dobbins, the headmaster, and he is very strict," she said. "This way."

"Where are we going?" Ricky asked.

"To my classroom. It's by the office."

"Don't we have to go down the hall to the left, then?" Billy asked.

"No, the office is straight ahead." Amy pulled them forward.

Isn't that the library? No, wait, that's in my time. Her office is-was-where my library is. Will be? Whatever. He shook his head. Time travel sure was confusing.

They heard voices behind them. "Someone's coming," Ricky said.

"Quick, in here," Amy said. She pushed the boys into a dark classroom. Billy looked around and spied a calendar on the wall. He leaned over an old wooden desk with an ink well. October 1954. He exchanged an incredulous glance with Ricky, who stood up and cleared his throat.

"Ummm, Amy, how do we get back to *our* time?" he asked in a squeaky voice.

"Shhh!" She covered her mouth and pointed to the open doorway. Billy peered around the corner into the hall.

A grey-haired man in a dark suit stood gesturing to some students in front of the library. Behind them, he could see Mr. Dobbins walking up to them.

"Amy, who is this guy?" Billy asked, popping his head back around. She glanced around the corner.

"That's Mr. Maynard, the art teacher."

"The one who painted the pictures in the gym, right?"

"Yes. He's talking to Mr. Dobbins."

"Let me see," Ricky said.

"Mr. Maynard, did you happen to see three students come down the stairs just now?"

"No, Headmaster. Do you know who they are?"

"That's just it. I didn't recognize two of them, two boys."

"And who was the other one?"

"I think she is in Mrs. Brown's grade seven class, but I don't recall her name. Are they with your group?"

"I don't believe so." Mr. Maynard scratched his head. "I'll have to check with the others upstairs."

Mr. Dobbins raised his eyebrows and tapped his cane on the floor. "Yes, well, these three didn't stop when I told them to."

"That doesn't sound like *my* students, Headmaster." Mr. Maynard glanced at the three boys and two girls standing beside him. They nodded their heads in agreement.

The headmaster frowned. "And how would you know if you're not watching them, sir?"

Mr. Maynard rubbed his hands together and cleared his throat. "My students know how to respect their elders, Mr. Dobbins. I assure you."

"They had better, sir." Mr. Dobbins scowled and spat the words out. "I want to know who those students are, and I want to talk to them before this night is over."

Maynard sighed heavily. "Yes, but if they are Mrs. Brown's pupils, shouldn't you be speaking with her?"

Dobbins rapped his cane on the floor, causing the students to jump back. "I have better things to do than round up students, Mr. Maynard. I am charging you with finding these students. Now you had better go and set up for the play."

The principal swished his cane at them as if to direct them away. The art teacher cleared his throat again, spun around on his heel, and strode toward the stairs. "Come on, children. Let's get the stage ready." The students followed him. Amy, Ricky, and Billy popped their heads back into the room just in time. The footsteps carried on down the hall and up the stairs. Billy peeked back around the corner. Mr. Dobbins was gone, too.

"Amy, how do we get back to our own time?" Ricky asked again.

"We have to go back to the vortex," she said. "There are two in the school, one in the gym and one in the boiler room, in the basement."

"Vortex? What's that?" Billy asked.

"It's a place where the past, present, and future are joined, and you can travel to different times."

"How do you know where it is?" Ricky asked.

"The orb shows me where to look."

"What orb?" Billy asked.

"This one." Amy pulled the shiny sphere out of her pocket.

"Wow." Billy stopped fingering the ink well and stared at it.

"My grandma gave it to me. She has had it for years. My great-grandma gave it to her when she was a little girl. It comes from a place called Salem, Massachusetts. That's where some witches were killed in 1692."

"Witches?" Ricky asked. "Oh, great."

"How did your great-grandma get it?" Billy asked.

"Some of the people who were practicing witchcraft escaped and moved up north to Canada. A lot of them practiced white magic, not black, Ricky. They were good witches. My great-great-great-grandma was one of them. She was a young girl when she came to New Brunswick. I'm descended from a long line of witches, and a lot of them came from Massachusetts."

"Okay," Billy said, "but how does the ogler orb work?"

"It's an 'ocular orb,' Billy. It works by creating a force that bends time and space, bringing them real close together so that a person can travel through a kind of tunnel to another time."

"How do you know where you're going?" Ricky asked.

"You can see through it before you activate it. It's like looking through a window. When I first came to your time, I scanned ahead. My grandma told me that there was a connection with the future, which would help me solve the mystery."

Billy raised his eyebrows. "Whoa, Amy, slow down. What are you talking about?"

"And what mystery?" Ricky asked. He leaned forward, eyes like golf balls.

"That's the scary part. Kids are missing, and nobody knows how or why. I've seen some creepy stuff, but I need your help to find out what's going on."

"What kind of creepy stuff?" Billy asked.

"That's what I want to show you, but we have to go to the basement."

"But how do we get back to our time?" Ricky asked.

"The vortex upstairs will take us back."

"I'd kind of like to see what's in the basement," Billy said.

Ricky raised his eyebrows. "Can't we see it another time?"

"I don't know, Ricky. I think this is kind of cool," Billy said. He smiled at Amy.

"Good," said Amy, twirling her hair. "We have to wait for the concert to be over first anyway."

"Oh, come on, Ricky. We'll get back. Quit worrying," Billy said.

"Okay, but not too long, all right, Amy?"

"Trust me, Ricky, when we return, they won't even know we've been gone. Come on. Follow me." She led them out into the hall toward some stairs at the other end of the school.

CHAPTER EIGHT

The Boiler Room

"This is the basement." Amy led them down a narrow hallway with white brick walls. "Nobody comes down here except the janitor, and he's busy helping with the set up for the concert." Billy looked down the dark, dirty hallway and smelled the same musty odor he noticed in the gym.

"It sure smells different from the basement in our school," he said.

"Where does that door go?" Ricky asked. He pointed to a small doorway on their right, almost embedded in an outcropping of rock.

"To a covered area where we play when it rains," Amy said.

"Our basement doesn't have rock in it either," Billy said.

"Where's that heat coming from?" Ricky asked. "From the boiler room. That's where we're going."

They stopped in front of a heavy metal door. "Help me open it." The boys pushed on it while Amy turned the doorknob. It did not budge an inch.

"What's with this door?" Billy asked.

"I don't know. It opens without a problem most of the time," she said. "Let's try again." The boys braced themselves against the metal door like linebackers, and Amy turned the knob. "Ready? Push!"

"Whoa," Billy cried as the door swung open, and a blast of heat washed over his face. A small light bulb swung from the ceiling and shone on some wooden steps that they scrambled down just before the door slammed shut.

"Man, it's hot in here!" Ricky said, looking back at the door. He sighed with relief when he saw the doorknob.

"That's why it's called a boiler room." Billy smiled at his friend.

"It's also a good place to hide," Amy said, pulling a little chair from against the wall and sitting down. Not seeing any other chairs, Billy sat on the steps, and Ricky followed suit. Billy

43

shuddered in the small room. It was about half the size of a classroom and filled with janitor stuff: mops, brooms, boxes of paper towels, rakes, a couple of old vacuums, and the odors of bleach and ammonia. The light barely pierced the dark, leaving the back of the room in shadow.

To the right of the boiler, yellow slickers hung on hooks with black peaked caps over the tops of them. "What are those rain jackets for?" he asked.

"Those are for the patrol kids who stand at the crosswalks. See the flags with the word 'stop' on them?"

"Oh, yeah. Are you a patrol kid?"

"No, but some of them are in my class."

"My grandpa told me that he was a patrol kid when he went to school." *He went*— Billy froze as the realization struck him like a kick in the gut. His grandfather was a kid in this school now, right this very minute. He could even be in a classroom just above his head. *I wonder if Amy knows him?* Billy opened his mouth to ask and then closed it again. He looked at the dusty ceiling with cobwebs hanging from the pipes and shivered.

"Are you okay?" Amy asked.

"Yeah, I don't like this small room, that's all."

The light bulb over their heads flickered.

"Maybe we shouldn't be here," Ricky said. He watched the light and shadows dance and clutched the handrail. "Amy, why don't we use the vortex in here to get back?"

"I tried, but for some reason, I can't get it to work."

Ricky gave him a worried look. "That's...too bad," Billy said, his shallow breaths showing his fear.

"Are you sure you're okay?" she asked him.

He inhaled a deep breath, trying to slow his breathing. "Yeah, I'm okay. What were you going to show us?"

"I brought you down here because this is where I saw one of the kids."

"What kids?" Billy asked, still surveying the room.

"The ones I told you about, the ones who are missing."

He met her eyes and leaned forward. "And you saw the kid here?"

"Not exactly, I followed him down the stairs, but when I opened the door, he wasn't here."

"You sure he didn't just go up the other stairs?" Ricky asked.

"He might have, but I thought I heard the door shut behind him."

"Did you recognize him?" Billy asked.

"Yes. His name was Derek, and he was in grade four."

"What did the teachers say?" Billy asked. The boiler grumbled like it had indigestion. The boys both stared at it, Billy waiting for it to say *excuse me*.

"That he just ran away," she said.

"Maybe he did," Ricky said.

"I don't think so. He was happy at school."

"Maybe he wasn't happy at home," Billy said.

"But, I heard his mom talking. She said there were no problems, and he didn't take any of his clothes or money with him. Does that make sense?"

"No."

"And there are other kids missing?" Ricky asked, tapping his fingers on the rail.

"Yes, just last month, Tommy went missing. He was a nice quiet kid."

"So what?"Billy said, frowning. "Nice quiet kids, don't go missing?" Amy sighed.

"What do the police think?" Ricky asked.

"They think that the kids just ran away, too."

"Without their things or money? They wouldn't get far." He shuffled his feet along the stair.

"Are you sure that these kids aren't just at a relative's or something?" Billy asked, chewing his lip.

"I don't think so. Their parents would have said something."

"Okay, but a couple of kids missing doesn't make a crime," he argued.

She sighed. "I know, but Tommy's sister, Karen, said none of his special stuff was missing, like his favorite badges from cowboy shows on TV."

"My grandpa used to watch those shows," Billy said.

"Maybe he left in a hurry," Ricky said.

Amy moaned. "Karen said that he would never leave without his special stuff."

"Yeah, that's like my sister and her stuffed animals; they're inseparable," Billy said.

"Maybe his parents are separated, and his dad kidnapped him," Ricky said.

Amy screwed up her face. "Why would he do that?" she asked.

"It happens all the time, Amy. Parents break up and fight over who gets the kids, and sometimes one of them kidnaps them."

Amy shook her head. "No, it doesn't."

"Well, how about some weird relative?" Ricky continued. "My dad says most of the time when kids go missing, a relative is involved. You know, like a bad uncle."

Amy frowned at him. "I don't think so."

"Then what happened to them?" Billy asked.

Amy raised her hands in the air. "I don't know, but they didn't just leave with a relative."

Billy and Ricky stared at each other without saying a word. "I don't know, man." Ricky shook his head. Billy took a deep breath and turned toward the furnace. *What did happen to them?*

Amy continued. "I heard some teachers talking, and one of them said that a weird guy used to hang around the grounds after school. He gave kids candy and stuff. Maybe he took them."

Ricky stood and paced around the little room. "This guy who hung around the school— when was the last time you saw him?"

"He was there last week."

Ricky stopped and eyed her. "Is there anyone else you have suspicions about?"

"My friend, Margaret, says that Mr. Smithers, the owner of the grocery store, is creepy. He always smells like booze, and he smiles and winks at her. He asks her if she would like some candy or to see what he has in the back. She says he makes her feel yucky."

"He sounds pretty creepy to me," Billy said.

"And then there's old Mr. Rungrind; he's the gardener at the Pooly Mansion across the street. He always yells at the kids when they go into his garden and says he's going to get them."

"He just sounds mean."

"I guess so." She hung her head and sighed. "Oh, wait—there's Mr. Cruikshank, the night janitor. He is somewhat strange, always complaining about the kids making a mess, and he never smiles. He stands outside the girl's P.E. changing room and eyes us like we're something good to eat."

"That's creepy, but that doesn't make him a kidnapper," Billy said, still trying to wrap his head around this new information. He sat and stared at the furnace and chewed his fingernails.

Ricky rubbed his hands together. "Yeah, there are weirdos in every neighborhood," he said. "Remember Mr. Forner, Billy? He used to sneak around the houses and peek into the windows until my dad caught him."

"Amy, the kid that went missing—the one you saw—" Billy said.

"Derek. His name was Derek."

"Did you look for him in this room?"

"No. I didn't have a chance. The janitor came in, and I had to leave. Why?"

"If he was in here, maybe we can find something of his to prove it."

"That's a good idea. Let's look," Ricky said, heading toward the wall to the right. Amy and Billy joined him, and they were soon busy turning over boxes and looking in the corners of the room.

After several minutes, Amy piped up. "I don't think there's anything here, guys. We should head back."

Billy brushed a cobweb out of his face. "Yeah, I guess you're right," he said.

"Hold on. I think I found something," Ricky said. Dust and dirt swirled into the air when he raised a blue cardigan from the floor.

Amy reached for it. "Let me see that." She took it from Ricky, shook it, and held it up by the collar. "This is Derek's sweater. I think it was his favorite because he wore it all the time. Look, it's ripped." She put her fingers through a large hole in the front of it. Just then, the furnace banged, and something rattled. Ricky jumped back against the wall.

"Whoa, that's weird," Billy said, backing toward the stairs.

"Bring the sweater and let's get out of here," Ricky said, joining Billy on the stairs. The light flickered. Ricky clung to the doorknob as if it was a life preserver. Billy placed his hand on Ricky's shoulder and glanced around the room. "I think someone is watching us," he said.

"Come on, you guys!" Ricky rattled the doorknob.
Amy squeezed the sweater and hopped up the stairs.

Ricky yanked on the doorknob, but it would not move. "Crap!" He wiped the sweat from his face. "Billy, help me with this door."

"Sure. You okay?"

He let go of the doorknob and wiped his hands on his pants. "I'll feel a lot better when we're out of here." Billy grabbed onto his friend. "I know what you mean," he said. Ricky turned the doorknob again. It still would not open. "One more time on my go. One, two, three!"

This time it opened with a whoosh, and they darted into the hall. The door slammed shut behind them. *The room is happy to be rid of us, too.*

"I'm glad we're out of there," Ricky said, wiping his face again.

"Me, too," Billy said. They made their way upstairs to the gym. A stream of people funneled down the main stairs, and the upper hall was crowded. Once in the gym, some kids, parents, and teachers stood in front of the stage talking.

"Follow me," Amy whispered, leading them behind the stage to the right."Wait until everybody is out of the gym. Here, Billy, hold this." She handed him the sweater and then took the orb out and waved her hand over the shiny little screen.

It's like a spherical cell phone. "What are you doing?" Billy asked.

"Setting it to the correct time and place. Ricky, check the gym." Ricky walked over to the stage curtain and peered through an opening.

"All clear," he said when he stepped back.

"Ready?" she asked. Billy and Ricky nodded their heads. She waved her hand over it and whispered, "*Oculus me ad futurum.*" She put the orb back in her pocket. "Take my hand."

Billy gulped. He and Ricky grabbed her hands. The wind surrounded them again, and everything went black. An invisible force reached out and hauled them away into a dark tunnel. Like before, there was no air, no light, just nothingness.

Minutes later, his lungs aching, Billy squeezed Amy's hand, willing her to do something.

Light and air burst in as the floor slammed up to meet his feet. He sucked in the sweet oxygen and fell forward with Amy and Ricky sprawled out in front of him. The smell was fresh, and the gym was clean; no paintings, no posters or jerseys on the floor. The balls were in their wire baskets, and the stage curtains were still.

"Ah!" Billy sighed in relief. They were back in his time.

"Are we back?" Ricky asked. He leaned up against the wall and rubbed his eyes.

"Yes, of course," Amy said, matter-of-factly, as if this happened every day. She stood up, stretched, and ran her fingers through her hair. "Follow me." On their way out, Billy picked up the sweater he had dropped and glanced back to the windows. The Venetian blinds were there, still hanging in their strange new geometry.

"What time is it?" Ricky asked.

"My watch says 11:15." Billy tapped the crystal and looked again in disbelief. "That means that we were only gone about five minutes."

"That's impossible," Ricky said. "It felt like hours."

"Well," Amy said. "Time slows down when you travel through the vortex, and you can come back almost to the exact time that you left."

"What?" Billy said. "That's convenient."

"I know," she said with a grin.

"One other thing I'd like to know. What does that *'Oculus prago or futuro whatever'* mean?"

"*'Oculus me ad praeteritum'* and *'oculus me ad futurum'* are spells. It's Latin and means 'With the eye, I wander through time and space' or something like that. My grandmother told me."

"Wow, that's pretty cool."

"Yeah, right," Ricky said. "Let's head back to class."

CHAPTER NINE

Voices

"What skills are required for good readers?" Mr. Moore asked.

Sally Ferguson said, "Good readers sound out words they don't know."

"Meddlers will be dealt with." Billy shivered at the low, bass voice and looked around. It was a man's voice. The only man here was Mr. Moore, and that was not his voice.

"Good readers figure out the meanings of words from the sentence," said another student.

"Obey, or there will be consequences." Billy looked around the classroom again. None of the kids moved. He held his breath, and his heart raced. Who was talking to him? Was he going nuts?

"Good readers can identify parts of speech," somebody else said.

"Listen to my speech."

"What?" Billy said aloud. The kids turned to look at him. His face flamed, and he wished he could drop through the floor. "Excuse me," he said. "Mr. Moore, may I go to the washroom, please?"

On his way out, he winked at Ricky. He shook his head as he walked down the hall. Did he imagine it? By the stairs, a freezing gust of wind hit him without any warning. He stopped and shivered.

"This is your only warning."

Billy shrieked and whirled around but saw no one. "Who are you?"

"You don't need to know."

"O-okay, okay," Billy stammered. His face flushed, and his heart thumped as if he had run a marathon. He scurried to the washroom and grabbed the sink with shaky hands. The sweat dripped from his nose as he opened the tap and splashed cold water onto his face and hair. His stomach heaved, and he gazed at his white face in the mirror.

"You okay?"

Billy screamed and spun around. "Oh, it's you." He slumped against the sink, shaking as Ricky approached him.

"What's wrong?"

"I...I keep hearing a voice inside my head saying awful things."

"What?" Ricky stared at his friend.

"Maybe I'm going crazy."Billy sighed and shook his head.

Ricky chewed his lip. "What's going on?"He shifted his feet back and forth.

Billy wrenched paper towels from the dispenser and wiped his face. "I keep hearing a man's voice yelling at me."

"You look freaked out, man."

"You would be, too," he said as he flung the paper into the bin.

Rubbing his arms, Ricky gulped. "What is the voice saying?"

Billy turned and looked in the mirror, gripping the sink edge until his knuckles turned white like the porcelain. He caught his friend's gaze and held it. "To watch my step, stop meddling, and stay out of it. Someone is threatening me."

"Hold on." Ricky put his hand on his friend's shoulder. "We've been through a lot of weird stuff today."

Billy's face flushed in anger. "You don't believe me. I heard a voice, okay?"

"Maybe you're just tired, man."

"I'm not just tired!" Billy shook him off and splashed water onto the mirror and wall in frustration. "It was real."

Ricky backed off and leaned against the wall. "Take it easy, man."

"No, I won't take it easy." He grabbed the sink and stared at his friend. "I don't know if I can do this. First, the fight with Andrew, then the crows, time travel, the missing boys, and now I'm hearing a terrible voice in my head. It's driving me crazy." Ricky just stared back at him as he continued. "Maybe we should just leave it alone. For all we know, Amy could be making all of this up."

"But all of that stuff happened to me, too."

Billy faced his friend. "We really went back in time, right?"

"Yes. We saw that calendar."

"And we saw those murals."

"Yes."

"And we found that sweater."

"Yes."

Billy stood quiet for a minute and looked at the floor. "But you don't hear the voice, do you."

"No." Ricky gave him an apologetic look. "But it doesn't mean you're crazy. I bet Amy knows more than she's telling us."

"There's no more to tell."

Billy jumped and stared at his friend, who stood stiff, his eyes like saucers. "You heard that, didn't you?" he demanded.

Ricky nodded his head and licked his lips. "Who is that?"

"I don't know, but you heard him, too. So maybe I'm not going crazy."

Ricky gulped. "Either that or we're both losing it."

"I really think we have to talk to Amy."

--*-*-*

Back in class, the kids were working quietly at their desks. Billy picked up a sheet of paper on his desk and scanned it. "People had to walk everywhere and ride horses or bicycles in the past. Life was slower, and they"—*sure didn't know about wormholes, or vortexes, or girls who could zap you from here to the past in the space of three breaths. That's travel, boy—time travel.*

The disturbing voice spoke again. **"You had better just stay where you are."**

"Stop it!" Billy yelled. Everyone stared at him. "Ah, sorry," he said. "I was just thinking out loud." He groaned, his face flushed, and he sank into his chair. Ricky sat rigid, his face white, eyes like circles. He had heard the voice, too. *At least I am not the only nut case.*

"Are you okay, Billy?" Mr. Moore asked. "Do you need to leave the room to figure it out?"

"No. I just got carried away, sir." He wiped his damp forehead.

Mr. Moore raised his eyebrows. "Well, you need to settle down then."

"Yes, sir." He choked on his words as he looked around the room. Sally Ferguson and a few other girls giggled and shook their heads. He sighed, his cheeks burning. Becky Ronson rolled her eyes, and Alex circled his ear with his finger. All of the boys laughed. All except Ricky, who just stared back at him with a pale, frightened face. Well, at least he would have a friend in the loony bin.

The lunch bell rang, and Billy almost jumped out of his seat. He dashed out without waiting for Ricky.

Outside, Ricky caught up with him by the big rock. "You okay?" he asked.

"I guess so. How about you?"

"I was fine until I heard that weird voice again."

"I know. Look, we have to find Amy."

"There she is, over by the little kids' playground." They rushed over and pulled her away from the slide.

"Hey, you guys. Slow down. What's up?" she complained. They hauled her to a secluded spot by the trees.

"Amy, I don't think you've told us everything. Some weird man's voice is in my head, and he's threatening me. What's going on?" Billy said, holding her arm.

She raised her eyebrows. "A voice in your head? Are you sure?"

"Yes, I'm sure. Ricky hears it, too."

Amy looked at Ricky, who nodded his head. "Okay, I'll tell you what I know. The boys have gone missing in my time, but when I come to your time, someone or something is watching me."

"What do you mean?" Billy asked.

"When I come through the vortex, I notice a shadow sometimes, but when I go back to my time, I don't see it."

"What does it look like?" Ricky asked.

"Human, I think, but the features are blurry, and I only see it for a second before it disappears."

"Do you think that's what is in my head?"

"I don't know." Amy rubbed her hands on her skirt. "There's something else I need to tell you."

"What?"

Amy looked around to make sure they were still alone. "Once, when I saw the figure, it looked like it was holding something that glowed. When I stared at it, my head hurt, and I got dizzy."

"Do you remember what the object was?" Billy asked, remembering his experience with the figure in the upper window.

"No, but I remember being dizzy and turning away. When I looked back, it was gone."

"Was it like a laser beam?" Ricky asked.

"What's that?" she asked.

"It's a light beam that is very powerful and can ac- actually burn through things," Ricky explained.

"It felt like it could burn my eyes. That's for sure," Amy said. "But I think this figure is using some kind of magic."

"Magic?" Ricky shook his head.

"Yes, magic," she said. "Remember when I told you that my great-great grandma came from Salem?"

"Yeah, so?"

"Well, my grandma still uses magic. If I ask her, she might know of a spell we can use to stop this thing in your head."

"What? Are you serious?" Ricky asked, raising his voice.

Billy shook his head, looked at the big oak beside them, and sighed. "A magic spell from a witch? I don't think that's a good idea, Amy."

"But it can protect us," she said.

55

"We don't even know if the voice in my head and the figure you saw are the same person."

Amy grabbed the arm of his jacket. "But we've got to do something."

Billy shook free. "Look, I need time to think about this."

Amy looked at Ricky. He shook his head. "Come on, man. I've heard enough about ghosts and time travel, evil spirits and witches. Let's go." Ricky pulled Billy's arm, and they left Amy standing by the tree.

CHAPTER TEN

The Ritual

Over the weekend, Ricky and Billy went for a bike ride through the park, played soccer, and watched movies. They laughed so hard they rolled on the floor. But most of all, they didn't once hear that awful voice in their heads. Billy all but forgot about Amy and time travel.

As they walked to school Monday morning, the cool September weather could not dampen Billy's spirits. They joked and teased while running through piles of leaves left by the wind. Near the school, the boys buried each other in a huge mound. Billy chucked acorns at Ricky, who tackled him and rubbed leaves in his face.

"Yuck," he said, smelling dog urine. Ricky laughed and rubbed harder. Billy hauled him down and shoved his face into the leaves, but when he climbed the stairs to the school grounds, the hair on the back of his neck stood up. He stopped and gazed up at the roof. The joy and laughter drained out of him as several crows leaned over the edge and cawed. One large bird swooped down and perched in a tree just above his head. Billy shivered while the blackbird leaned over and cawed right in his face.

He jumped back. "What's with that stupid bird?"

"What? It's just a bird," Ricky said. Several crows circled over their heads.

"It's not just the birds. It's everything."

"What are you talking about, man?"

Billy groaned and then dropped his backpack. The birds squawked even louder. He covered his ears. "Shut up!" he shouted at the sky.

"Take it easy." Ricky reached for Billy's arm.

Billy shrugged him off. "I've had it with this crap."

"Hey, they're just stupid birds."

"But I'm tired of all of it, Ricky—the crows, Amy, threatening voices, missing boys—I'm sick of it."

"Me too, mate."

The big black crow continued to squawk. Billy sat on a cement ledge by the stairs and stared at it. "I'm done with it. Amy can solve her own problems."

"Good. Let's go play soccer. And hey, one more good thing."

Billy sighed and looked at his friend. "What?"

"Andrew didn't come after us. Remember? He said he would."

"Yeah, I guess he forgot."

"Oh, I didn't forget, puke face." Andrew rounded the corner of the building and leaned against the wall, arms folded on his chest. "I'm just waiting for the right moment." He laughed and nudged his friend, Damen, who snickered. The crow in the tree glided down and landed on Andrew's shoulder. He didn't even flinch.

Damen stepped back, his eyes wide. Billy stiffened and raised his eyebrows in disbelief.

"We're planning something special for you, puke boy," Andrew said. Damen snickered.

"What are you planning?" Mr. Moore stepped down the stairs. With a caw and a rustle of its wings, the crow flew off.

Andrew unfolded his arms. "We were just talking about what costume to wear for Halloween, sir."

"Is that right?" Mr. Moore eyed the boys.

"Yeah, Billy said he's going as Harry Potter," Andrew said.

"And Ricky's going as Hermione Granger," Damen mocked him.

Ricky snorted and glanced toward Mr. Moore. "Yeah, right, just like Andrew is going as Rumplestiltskin, and you're one of his witches, Damen." Billy snickered.

The vice principal looked back and forth between the boys. He raised his eyebrow and stared at Billy, who shrugged his shoulders. "We were just fooling around," Billy said.

Mr. Moore gave Andrew a stern look. "Andrew, Damen, come hold the doors for me."

"Yes, sir," Andrew answered. Sneering at Billy, he hopped up the stairs.

The bell rang. "Well, we had a good weekend anyway." Ricky threw his backpack over his shoulder. Billy nodded, grabbed his backpack, and they shuffled up the stairs. He ignored Andrew's triumphant smirk as they passed.

Hanging up his jacket, Billy glanced around the room. His entire body lightened with relief when he realized that Amy was not there. He could forget it all—it was over, and he would not have to deal with any more crazy stuff—tornadoes in the gym, time travelers, missing kids from the past or spooky voices in his head. He strode to his desk, ignoring Andrew, who was leaning back in his seat, feet on his desk, grinning like the Cheshire cat in the Alice books. Billy dropped into his chair and focused on the board behind Mr. Moore.

--*-*-*

After gym class, Billy stood at the top of the stairs gazing into the hallway. *It was nice to have a day without anything weird happening. Then again, what was with that crow on Andrew's shoulder?* Billy shook his head. *Nope, that's over. Done. I am finished with all of that scary stuff.* He turned just in time to notice a blond ponytail disappearing down the end staircase. *Is that Amy?* He squinted. *No, I am not*—he stiffened and snatched for the handrail when he felt a shove from behind. Toppling over, he missed, plummeting down the stairs, arms pinwheeling. He pivoted in the air, bounced, shoulders and arms smacking the wooden steps, and then rolled, hearing cries and screams above him but too busy falling to pay attention.

He grabbed again for the rail and caught it, his body twisting with the sudden change in momentum, pain exploding all through his legs when he whacked into the wooden stairs. The shock loosened his grip and he tumbled again, bouncing down—head, back, knees, until he thumped into a pair of legs.

He lay still, dazed, battered, and bruised. Pain shot through him from his feet to his head. It took a moment before he realized hands were gripping him, holding onto him. Nylon brushed against his arm, and he caught a whiff of a peachy scent like a perfume his mom wore sometimes. The world slowly stopped spinning, and he caught his bearings, recognizing the principal.

"Are you okay?" Ms. Fenton asked.

"I think so," he puffed, trying to catch his breath, his heart in his throat. Kids gawked down at him from the landing and up from the main floor. Excited voices babbled. "Did you see that? Did somebody push him? I thought he was going to go all the way down. He could have broken his neck."

"What happened, Billy?" the principal asked.

"I'm not sure. One minute I was standing on the landing, and the next minute I was falling."

"Let's get you back upstairs," she said, helping him up. "Are you sure you're all right?"

"Yes, I think so." He struggled with the rail and winced at the pain shooting through his wrist and shoulder.

"I saw the whole thing, Ms. Fenton," Ricky said from the top of the stairs. "Becky pushed him, and he fell."

"I didn't push him. Somebody pushed me. I'm sorry, Billy. Someone knocked me into you."

"Someone knocked you into him?" Ricky's eyes narrowed.

"Yes." Becky turned on Ricky. "I was standing beside him when someone knocked me into him. I didn't do it on purpose!" Tears spilled from her eyes.

"What?" He scoffed, his hands in the air. "I saw it. You bumped into him. There wasn't anyone else around."

Becky stamped her foot and trembled as tears streamed down her cheeks. "It was an accident."

"I can't believe you're saying that." Ricky pointed his finger at her. "He fell because of you."

The principal stepped between them. "That's enough."

Ricky stepped back, frowning.

"But I didn't mean to, Ms. Fenton." Becky sobbed into her hands.

"I know. It was an accident. You just lost your balance and bumped Billy." The crowd of kids stood silent. " Everybody, back to class, please." The teachers rounded up their charges and headed back to their rooms.

Billy heard the kids muttering as they left the stairs and was relieved that he was not the center of attention anymore.

Ricky scowled as Becky bawled. "I really don't know what happened, Billy. I'm terribly sorry," she said between sobs.

"I know you didn't do it on purpose. I'll be okay," he said as he rubbed his shin.

"Let's have the nurse look at you," Ms. Fenton said, ushering him back down the stairs. "Becky, you'd better come, too, until you settle down a bit. Ricky, you go back to class."

--*-*-*

At recess, Billy limped out to the oak tree with Ricky. "Are you sure you're okay?" Ricky asked.

"Yeah, I'll live."

"Is something going on again? I mean, that was scary, and Becky didn't trip."

"I don't know, but if nobody else was there, who pushed her?"

"I did."

Billy froze. "I could have been killed." His cheeks chilled. "He's trying to kill me." Billy stared at Ricky, whose eyes widened, his face blanched. They locked eyes and held onto each other. Ricky's trembling arms told him that he thought so, too.

"Why?" Billy asked.

"You are part of this, and you cannot escape it."

"But I don't want any part of it."

"Too bad. You got yourself into it, and now, you will pay for it."

"But why us?" Ricky asked. The voice did not answer.

"I don't know what to do," Billy said.

"Maybe if we just leave it alone, he won't come after us anymore." Ricky looked hopefully to the sky, but the voice was silent.

"I don't think we have a choice. He's after us anyway. Maybe we need to talk to Amy again."

"But that'll probably just piss him off more."

"He tried to kill me. How much more pissed off can he get?"

"You're right, but why won't he leave us alone?"

"Maybe if we think about what's happened so far, we can figure it out." Billy looked at the tall oak tree. "This all started after we came back from Amy's time, right?"

"No, this started with the first day of school. Remember? You saw that guy in the window."

"Yes, of course. That means this spirit has been after me from the beginning." Billy grabbed his friend by the shoulders. "That's why he won't leave me alone. He's afraid of *me*."

"I don't think so. Come on. He's an evil spirit, and you're just a thirteen-year-old kid."

"I know; I mean, he must be afraid of something about me." Billy screwed up his face in frustration. "It doesn't make sense."

"Maybe it's because of something else that's happened."

Billy gazed back at the school. "Yeah, but what?"

"I don't know."

"Okay, after the window, Andrew went weird, and we fought him."

"Then the crows attacked us."

"And Amy took us back to her time."

"We saw the murals," Ricky said.

"Uh huh, and we ran into the headmaster, Dobbins."

"We saw Max Maynard."

"Then we went to the boiler room and found one of the missing kid's sweaters."

"Do you think bringing back that sweater has caused all this fuss?"

"Maybe, but I think there's something else we're missing. Do you think the spirit knows that we've talked to Amy?"

"Probably—if he's listening now," Ricky said. They both looked skyward.

"And maybe Amy knows what we're missing. There's got to be some connection between her and us that will make sense of it."

"Well, what should we do then?"

"We need to talk to Amy again. I thought I saw her just before I fell down the stairs. Maybe she's back in our time."

"But what is she going to tell us?"

"I don't know, but she must know more than we do."

"It's also got to be linked to those lost kids somehow, because that's the only thing that we found out about, right?"

The bell rang, and kids ran for the door. "Later," Billy said as they headed for the door, too.

--*-*-*

Billy glanced at the clock. Time was running out, and the score was tied. He reached in to knock the ball free from Andrew's grasp.

"Pass the ball. Shoot. Stop him, Billy." He ignored his teammates and reached in again. Andrew bounced it just out of reach and pushed back against him. Billy's runners squeaked as he stumbled backward, and he froze when Andrew turned and stared him down. Billy shuddered as the brown eyes flashed into glowing yellow orbs, and Andrew's elbow caught him in the temple. Everything went black.

When he came to, his head ached. Through his blurred vision, he saw Mr. Moore kneeling beside him and hazy faces gawking down.

"You okay, Billy?" Mr. Moore asked.

"Yeah, I think so," he mumbled and rubbed his eyes. His vision cleared, and he sat up.

"That was a bit of a shot you took there." Mr. Moore helped Billy to his feet. "Andrew, you need to keep your elbows under control."

Andrew screwed up his face. "I didn't hit him," he said, still bouncing the ball. "Billy fell down trying to check me."

Billy caught his gaze and stared in disbelief as the boy's eyes glazed over and then glowed yellow for just an instant. Billy went rigid. Andrew winked. Billy gulped, drew in his breath, and surveyed his classmates, but no one else seemed to notice. *Am I seeing things?*

--*-*-*

After school, on their way to the gate, Billy asked, "Ricky, in the gym today, did you notice anything strange about Andrew's eyes?"

"No. Why?"

"They changed color for a second, to yellow, like an animal's."

"Are you sure?" Ricky raised an eyebrow. "You took a pretty hard knock to the head."

"I know what I saw. It happened before the hit in the head and again when I woke up. The same thing happened when I was fighting with him."

Ricky stopped at the gate, leaning against the post to the chain-link fence and looked past the cement steps that led to the street. "Yeah, he was pretty freaky that day."

"I really think something is wrong with him."

"He is just fine, but you're not."

"Get out of my head!" Billy shouted. He threw his backpack off, sat on the steps, and watched the cars stream by.

"Easy, mate. Everyone is looking at you."

Billy looked up. Several kids stared as they passed. "Are you okay?" A familiar voice spoke from behind him. He turned around.

"Amy. You're back." Billy rose to greet her. "I thought you were gone for good." Relief and anxiety flooded him at seeing her again. *If she helped them fight this evil spirit, it would be a good thing. On the other hand, if her coming here caused the spirit to attack them, then it was bad, really bad. What should I do?*

"I thought so, too, but those boys are still missing. We have to help them."

"**You cannot help them**."

Billy started at the voice. He stared at Amy, who looked like she had been caught stealing something. "Did you hear that?" he asked.

"Yes, I did," she said, her face losing its color. She stepped aside when some kids pushed through.

Billy gulped and picked up his backpack. "Let's get out of the way," he said, starting down the steps.

"We have to help them, Billy," Amy said again. "We're the only ones who can."

"**I told you, you—**"

As Billy stepped through the gate, the voice broke off like a dropped cell phone call.

"There's got to be some way of—" Amy said.

"The voice stopped," Billy cut her off, his eyes widening.

"What?" Amy asked.

"Maybe he can't hear us off the school grounds."

"Let's make sure," Ricky said. "You can't stop us."

No voice answered.

"You can't touch us," Billy said. Still no response.

"Get lost, evil dude," Ricky said. Silence.

"I want to be absolutely certain," Billy said, stepping back up the stairs and through the fence. "Why can't we help them?"

"**They are beyond—**"

Billy jumped back outside the fence, and the voice cut out.

"It works. He can't get into our heads beyond the school grounds," he said.

"He probably can't hear us either," Amy said.

"That makes sense," Ricky agreed.

They sat on the cement wall, and Billy told Amy about the events of the day. She gasped and covered her mouth.

"Oh my God," she said, staring into Billy's eyes. "You could have been killed!"

Billy's throat tightened, and he blinked back tears. "I know." His voice trembled. He dropped his head and sat with his hands over his face, trying to push the horrific events of the day out of his mind, but it was too much.

Amy laid her hand on his shoulder. "I think I can help."

"I'm afraid of him, Amy," he said between sobs."I don't know if I can do this."

She rubbed his shoulders. "We can do it together."

"But why is he still after us?" His voice hitched. "Amy?" He wiped his face and glanced up at her. "We need to know what's going on."

She chewed her lip, nodded her head, and took a deep breath. "Well, I'm pretty sure that the evil spirit is from the past, my past." She stopped and gulped. "The boys disappeared in my time, so I think one of the adults from the school is responsible."

"Which one?" Billy asked.

"I don't know, maybe a teacher."

"But why would they do it?" Ricky asked.

"I don't know," Amy said. "But someone is trying to stop us from finding out what happened to the lost boys."

"But why are they worried about us? We're kids, and he's an evil spirit," Billy argued.

"Yeah, we don't know magic," Ricky said.

"But I do," Amy said, her eyes shining.

"How can you stop him?" Billy asked.

"We have to perform a protection spell."

"A what?" Ricky asked.

"It's a special ritual for protecting people from evil spirits."

"And it really works?" Billy asked.

"Yes, but you have to do exactly what I tell you to do, both of you." She eyed Ricky. "Or it won't work." She held the boys' hands in hers and gazed into their eyes. "Do you understand?"

"Yes, I get it," Billy said, relieved they could actually do something to get rid of this evil spirit.

"How about you, Ricky?"

"I don't think so. Look what happened to Billy today. It's too dangerous." He paced in a circle.

"If we don't do anything, it will get a lot more dangerous, and the evil spirit's power will grow," she said, eyeing him.

"He already tried to kill me," Billy said.

Ricky continued to pace. "But magic is dangerous, too. What if it doesn't work?"

"Then we try something else," she said. "Maybe we could tell someone," Ricky argued.

"But who will believe us?" she countered.

"My dad. No, forget it," Ricky said. "There's no other way?"

"I don't think so," Amy said. "We have to protect ourselves before it's too late."

Ricky kicked at the dirt with his runner. "I guess so, then."

"Okay, meet me back here tonight at midnight."

Billy started. "Why then?"

"It has to be at midnight with a full moon for the spell to work. There's a full moon tonight."

"But, do we have to come back to the school where the spirit is and can hear us?" Ricky asked.

"Yes, it has to be where the spirit is to affect him. Don't worry. I know how to do it."

Ricky started to pace again. "But what if he comes after us while we're doing it?"

"I'll take care of him. I know what I'm doing."

"I'm with you, Amy. Let's do it," Billy said. She looked hard at Ricky.

Ricky sighed deeply, frowned, and shook his head back and forth. "Me, too," he reluctantly agreed.

"Good. You have to bring some things. I can't give them to you, because they have to be yours to make it work. Write these down so you don't forget them."

She dictated a list, then grabbed their arms and stared at both of them. "I'll meet you under the front stairs at midnight."

--*-*-*

The dim moonlight peeked through the mist around the trees and bounced light and shadow on the cement path like a lamp in the fog. The red brick of the school smoldered like burnt coals while the glass in the bell tower shimmered. The cement steps below reflected the moonlight reminding Billy of headstones in a graveyard. The wind howled through the tall oaks like moaning ghosts, and dead leaves scratched like claws along the walkway. *Am I in a Dracula movie or something? I'm going to my doom.*

Ricky stopped and gulped when they approached the front stairs. "I don't know if this is such a good idea."

"We didn't come this far just to go back home," Billy said.

He took a deep breath and pulled his collar up to shield himself from the whipping wind. Amy rubbed her arms as she stood in front of the stairs, shivering.

"Are you okay, Amy?" Billy asked.

"I'll be all right. Did you bring everything?"

"Yes."

"Good," she said. "We're ready then. Bring it here." The boys followed her, and they huddled under the stairs. "I need the salt," Amy said. Billy reached into the bag and handed her a small container of salt. She poured it into a circle around them. Billy shuddered, thinking of that day when the crows attacked them. *Would they come again?*

"What time is it?" Amy asked.

Billy yanked his sleeve to free his watch and gazed at the glowing digits. "Eleven fifty-five," he said, his heart quickening.

"Good. Now place the candle in the center of the circle and light it."

Billy followed her directions. The light glowed and flickered in the gusts of wind.

"It has to keep burning. Ricky, block the passage so the wind doesn't blow it out," she said. Ricky stepped in front of the opening in the brickwork. The candle flickered but burned steadily, making the shadows dance on the back wall.

"Give me the wand and the blue ribbon." She wrapped the ribbon around the stick and faced the north corner of the circle, tapped the wand on the ground, and spoke. "I call thee, you who guard the watchtowers of the north, to guide me through the darkness and ensure my safety."

Billy gulped as the wind gusted and salt flew up into his eyes. It stung, and he winced. Amy faced south, tapped the wand, and said the same words. More salt blew up. He closed his eyes until the wind died down. She went through the ritual; the light from the candle glowed brighter. She swung to her left and spoke louder. Each time she repeated the phrase, he relaxed a little more, as if somebody was behind them, guiding her movements. He took a deep breath, and his fear melted away.

When she finished, Billy glimpsed a shadowy figure swirling out into the candle's glow. He glanced over at Ricky, who stared at Amy.

"Stop!"

Billy looked at the figure and then over to Amy. *Did she see it, too?* She did not move. A moment later, she continued speaking as if she had noticed nothing.

"You will not finish it."

Amy stopped talking. The ghostly image swelled in front of him just outside of the circle. His heart quickened when two yellow eyes glowed back at him. The figure grew larger and more human-like: a hollow face and toothless mouth with a few strands of gray-black hair on a bare skull. A boney hand reached out but could not cross the salt circle. Billy glanced at Amy, silent and still like a wax figure. He gulped his heart back down. *What's happened to her?*

"Amy," he whispered, grabbing her arm. It felt lifeless, wax-like, and cold as ice. "Amy?" Panic rose like bile in his throat. He shook her. The wand fell out of her frozen hand and clinked onto the cement. He glanced at Ricky, who stood like a stone statue as well. *How could he stop this?*

"Stop what you are doing. Now!"

Billy spun around. The gaunt, skeletal figure's eyes bored into his skull. A sharp pain shot through his head. He blinked, but the gruesome image stayed. The hollow eyes, nose holes, and lipless mouth looked like the grim reaper. His stomach rolled as the boney fingers reached toward him, and piercing pain shot through his brain. He fell to his knees and grabbed his head in agony. *Leave me alone.* The cane flashed like fire. His head throbbed as if roofers' hammers were pounding on it. Through his blinding agony, Amy reached down and picked up the wand.

"I will stop your pain if you end it."

Billy tried to scream, but a needle shot through his head, and fear froze his voice. "Get out of my head," he mouthed. Ricky jumped forward just as a gust of wind blew salt over them, and the candle went out.

"Quick, light the candle!" Amy shouted.

Billy, frozen and helpless in the cane's white glow, watched Amy step back into the center of the circle. The relit candlelight fought the wind, and the grisly figure pointed his fiery cane at him.

"It will not, must not be done," the spirit said.

Amy's voice answered over the howl of the wind. "It will be finished, and you with it."

"You cannot stop me. You and your friends will be silenced."

The creature raised his cane like a torch and aimed it at her. The wind whipped salt into their faces, but the candle burned steady.

Amy stood firm and pointed the wand at the figure. "In the shadows, evils hide, ready to draw me from love's side, but with your help, I shall be strong and banish all who do me wrong."

"**You shall not**," the man commanded and thumped his cane on the stone underneath him. A whirlwind blew the salt, and the supplies against the walls, and the candle flickered.

Amy winced, but continued. "And banish all, who—"

"**It ends now!**" The spirit shouted and thumped the cane harder. The grotto glowed bright, the candle went out, and a bolt from his cane struck Amy. She screamed and collapsed, the wand falling from her hand as the glow and the spirit disappeared.

Energy flowed back into Billy's body like electricity. "Amy!" He grabbed her lifeless form, but she did not respond.

"Is she okay?" Ricky asked, stepping forward. Amy moaned.

"Are you okay?" Billy asked. His hands trembled, and tears welled up in his eyes. "We shouldn't have done this."

"What happened?" She groaned and rubbed her head.

"The evil spirit zapped you with his cane," Billy said.

Ricky leaned over her.

"I don't feel so good," she said.

Billy helped her sit up. "Take it easy."

She groaned again. "I didn't finish it. If it hadn't been for you, he would have..."

"It's okay, Amy. Can you walk?" His voice trembled.

"I think so, but I'm dizzy. I feel sick. We'll have to find another way to beat him."

"As long as you're okay," Billy said.

"Thank goodness I heard your voice. I've got to get back."

"How are you going to do that?"

"With the ocular orb." She brushed off her clothes and tried to stand.

"Are you sure you're all right?" Ricky asked, helping pull her to her feet.

"I'll be okay if I get back to Grandma. She'll take care of me. You and Ricky get home before anything else happens." They stepped out of the grotto, Amy holding the wall and Billy for support. Ricky picked up the remains of their equipment and followed them.

Amy set the orb and stepped halfway up the stairs.

"Be careful," Billy said. She disappeared in a whirlwind.

CHAPTER ELEVEN

The Lion's Head

The next morning Billy sat on the wall waiting for Ricky. He went over and over what Amy had said, "If it hadn't been for you." *How did I help her? Unless she heard my thoughts. Nah, it's just her imagination. I didn't do anything.* Billy yawned and looked up at the school's roof shining in the sun. A small group of crows cawed as they flew off the bell tower and landed in the tall oak tree above him, welcoming him back.

"How are you doing?" Ricky asked as he came up the sidewalk.

Billy turned around. "Okay, I guess," he answered. "Do you think I helped Amy last night?"

"No. How could you? You don't know magic."

"I guess so, but I was trying to help her."

"So was I, dude, but it doesn't mean we did anything."

"But, she said I did."

"Forget about it. Are you ready for Halloween?" Billy nodded and listened to the birds chirping.

"Do you think she's okay?"

"I don't know, but I bet that spirit is mad after last night. I wonder if he gets stronger around Halloween."

"Yeah, probably." Billy was still worried about Amy. "Too bad we screwed up the ritual."

"We didn't screw it up." Ricky shook the chain-link fence. "Amy did. She's the one who screwed up."

"But we did it together."

"Yeah, so, thanks to her, Mr. Evil is even more pissed off with us."

Billy's anger flared. "She tried her best. Stop blaming it all on her."

"But it was her idea, and she said she could do it."

"I wish we had some way of going back to Amy's time to find out if she's okay."

"What?" Ricky grabbed the fence again. "I don't think so. That's what made it worse, to begin with, remember?"

"I know. I'd just like to know how she's doing."

"After that shot she took, she might be seriously hurt, maybe in the hospital."

"I hope not. She tried so hard to defeat him," Billy said, tears welling up.

Ricky sighed. "Yeah, well, she didn't, and it didn't help, did it."

Billy scowled. "At least she tried."

"She shouldn't have offered if she couldn't do it."

"Okay, I get it," Billy said sharply, "but I'd still like to go back to see her somehow."

"But how?" Ricky scoffed. "We don't have an ocular orb."

"I know, but we still need to find out why the spirit is after us."

"You girls waiting for the bell?" Andrew asked from behind them.

Billy hopped off the wall, and Ricky spun around. Andrew and Damen stood with their hands in their pockets.

"What's it to you?" Ricky asked, stepping forward.

"Get out of my face, dick." Andrew shoved him backward. Damen snickered as Ricky bounced against the fence and stepped forward with clenched fists.

"Give it a rest, Andrew." Billy held Ricky back. "Another fight, and you'll be suspended for a month."

"I don't give a—" Andrew started, but before he could finish, a soccer ball bounced off his back.

"Whoops, sorry, man," a boy said from behind. "You guys want to play a game?" It was Jonathon from their class. Three other boys flanked him.

"Sure," Billy said, glad for the distraction. "Come on, Ricky." The boys left Andrew and Damen as they sped through the gate to the backfield.

"That was a close one," Billy said to Ricky when the bell rang.

--*-*-*

"Billy, Ricky, what animal are you going to research?" asked Mr. Moore.

"Lions, sir," replied Billy.

"Good choice, the school mascot. Jennifer and Amber, what animal?"

"Monkey," they both said. Some of the boys giggled. Mr. Moore continued asking all of the pairs until every group had chosen an animal. As soon as he gave the word, Billy and Ricky rushed to the computers at the back of the room.

"Google it," said Billy as Ricky positioned his fingers over the keys.

"Look at that," Ricky crowed. "Seventy-six million hits."

"We're not going to have any problem finding information, that's for sure."

"It says that lions are in the genus *Panthera* and the family *Felidae*."

"A lion is *Panthera Leo*; that's Latin." They scoured the computer sites. "Some male lions grow to be 250 kilograms."

"Wow, that's big." Billy peered over Ricky's shoulder. "And they live longer if they are in captivity, around twenty years instead of ten to fourteen."

Ricky clicked on another site. "Look, these are quotes from the Bible. One Maccabees 3 says, '*He was like a lion in his deeds, like a lion's cub roaring for prey.*'"

"Cool, and look at this one. Proverbs 30 says, '*the lion, which is mightiest among the beasts and does not turn back before any.*' Pretty neat, eh?"

"That's for sure. Look at this page. 'Lions in Mythology'. It says that Aker was one of Egypt's oldest lion gods. '*He guarded the gate of the dawn through which the sun god emerged every day.*'"

"I didn't realize that lions were so important," Billy said. As they scribbled down information, the bell rang for recess. By the

75

time they put their notebooks away, most of the class had already left.

--*-*-*

"Let's go the other way," Billy said, steering Ricky toward the office when he noticed Andrew and Damon by the exit door, eyeing them. In front of the library, Billy glanced back to see the two boys right behind them.

"Where are you boys going?" Mrs. Overon asked. "I forgot my book upstairs," Billy said, dodging to the right and up the staircase.

"We'd better find somewhere to hide." Ricky bounded up behind. "There, it's empty." He pointed to a classroom.

"Nowhere to hide," Billy said. "What about the can?"

"It's the first place they'll look."

Billy glanced over his shoulder. Luckily, Mrs. Overon was talking to their pursuers.

"The gym, quick." Inside, they stood still for a moment, looking around until they heard Andrew's voice in the hall.

"Under the stage," Billy whispered. They yanked the door open and ducked into the cupboard.

"It sure is dark in here," Ricky said.

"Shhh." Billy put his hand on his shoulder. The door clicked open, and footsteps came into the gym. The light, leaking in from the cracks, exposed dark piles of cloth and long skinny poles. The smell of polished wood mixed with rubber mats filled the space. He held his breath as footsteps squeaked across the polished wooden floor.

"They're not in here," Damen said.

"Maybe they went through the back," Andrew said. "Come on." Billy exhaled when he heard the back door click shut.

"That was close." Ricky reached under himself and removed a cloth bag with a lump in it. "This thing's digging into my butt." He opened the bag and pulled the lump out.

"Let me see," Billy said. He held it in the bar of light coming from the door. It was white, smooth, and cold in his hand. Ricky opened the door, and they scrambled out.

"Whoa," Billy said. "It's a lion's head."

"Pretty cool. *Panthera Leo.*" Ricky smiled and stretched.

Billy nodded. The object started to glow, warming his hand. "Look, it's glowing."

"Whoa, that's awesome."

"Maybe it's magic." Billy inspected it closely. It was made of ivory, with dirt in the carved mane. The eyes were blue crystals embedded in the face. "I wonder what Amy would say if she saw it?" He imagined her standing in the fifties gym with the murals surrounding her.

Ricky snickered, taking the Leo from Billy. "Prob- ably say it was her grandma's."

"*Panthera Leo.*" Billy took it back. The head glowed brighter and burned his hand. He grimaced and dropped it. The boys stood with their mouths open.

"Maybe the words '*Panthera Leo*' are the magic."

Mesmerized by the glow, his head whirling, the last thing Billy saw was the bright blue eyes of the Leo. Then everything went black.

He woke up sitting on the gym floor surrounded by First Nations murals. "Ricky," he howled, his eyes wide. "We went back in time."

"Must've been those words." Ricky rubbed his eyes and sat up.

"That head must be magical, but where is it?" He rose and scanned the stage.

"I don't see it." Ricky jumped up in a panic. "How are we going to get back?"

"We've got to find it." Billy ran all over the gym, moving chairs and swishing the curtains out of the way. Ricky rattled the window blinds. "It's got to be here somewhere." After several minutes, the boys sat on the stage dejected.

"Great. Now what do we do?"

"We find Amy."

77

"She might not even be in school today. Probably stayed home to stir her cauldron."

Billy ignored his comment."She's got to be here."

"I bet she's in the hospital after last night."

Billy frowned. "I doubt it. Even if she is at her house, how are we going to find it?"

"Good question."

Billy sighed and looked at the clock on the wall. "Let's make sure she's not here first. Ten fifteen. I wonder when recess is." As if in answer, the buzzer rang.

"What luck," Ricky said sarcastically. "Now it will be easier to find her. She'd better be able to help us get back."

"We have to try. She's our only hope. Let's head outside."

The playground looked the same, except there were no climbing apparatuses or a grassy field to play on. Kids swung on rope swings and slid down metal slides, but no Amy. Boys played marbles and shared baseball cards. Girls skipped, and others played hopscotch, but Amy was nowhere to be seen.

Billy screwed up his face. "Where is she?"

"There she is." Ricky pointed over by the rocks. She sat under a small tree with another girl.

"Amy," Billy called. Her head turned, and she looked at her friend for a moment before she rose and ran to meet them.

"H-hi, boys," she said, looking confused.

"Hi," Billy said. Ricky nodded.

"How did you get here?"

"We found this thing like a lion's head," Billy said.

"And when we said 'Panthera Leo,' it glowed and got hot," Ricky added. Amy raised her eyebrows.

"We said it again, and the next thing we knew, we were here," Billy explained.

"Wow," she said. "Do you have it with you?"

"No," Ricky said. "It didn't come with us like the ocular orb, so we can't get back to our time."

"That's why we had to find you," Billy said.

"We need to get back. If you can do it, that is." Ricky folded his arms.

"We wanted to know if you were okay, too." Billy put his hand on her shoulder.

"I'm a bit better since I talked to grandma. She gave me some healing herbs, and I had a deep sleep."

Ricky kicked at the dirt. "Can you take us back, then?"

Amy looked annoyed. "Yes, I can get you back, but we still have to talk about the spirit and the boys."

Ricky frowned. "Forget it, Amy. We just want to go home."

"Just a minute, Ricky," Billy said. "Amy, we've got a bunch of questions to ask you."

"Okay," she said as she sat on a bench.

"Why has this evil spirit attacked us from the beginning of the school year?"

"What do you mean?" she asked.

"He's been after Ricky and me since the first day of school. We think there's something about us that's making him attack us."

"Really? I don't know what."

"You don't? You sure knew a lot yesterday, didn't you? How come all of a sudden you don't know any- thing?" Ricky barked.

"I thought I knew what he wanted yesterday, but he's after something else."

"What else is there that we're missing?" Billy asked.

"Yes, Amy." Ricky spat the words out. "And what about last night? You said you had it all figured out."

"I'm sorry." Her head dropped. "I thought I could do it, but he was too strong."

"Yeah, and now we're in big trouble because of you and your stupid magic," Ricky snarled. Amy cupped her hands over her face.

"Hold on. It wasn't all her fault. Maybe we could've done more," Billy said.

"Like what?" Ricky demanded.

79

Amy wiped her eyes. "No, Billy, Ricky is right. I tried, and I failed. I'm sorry." She looked at Ricky expectantly. He frowned and turned away.

Billy looked back and forth between them, frustrated with Ricky's anger. He seized on the first thing that came to mind. "Amy, last night you said that I helped you. How?"

She wiped her eyes and looked up. "When I couldn't move, I heard your voice. I felt your strength, and it freed me from the spirit's control. If I'd been stronger, I would have defeated him."

"Yeah, right." Ricky raised his eyebrows.

She stared at him. "Yes. I could have done it with Billy's help."

"How?" Billy asked.

"By sharing your strength—your energy." She reached forward and grabbed Billy's arm. "That's what you did."

"Is this more of your magical bull?" Ricky asked in disgust.

Amy swung around and faced him. "Ricky, it's true!" He rolled his eyes.

"What about all of this other stuff that's happened?" Billy asked. Then he and Ricky told her about all of the weird things that had occurred since the beginning of the school year.

"If the spirit has been watching us all this time, he would know we're trying to figure it out," Ricky said.

"Maybe he knew you were going to interfere with his plans or something." Amy rubbed her skirt.

"He started speaking to us when we came back through time," Billy said.

"And threatening us," Ricky added."How else would he know?" He stared at her, challenging her.

"He might have used magic," she said. "There are many magical ways to see things."

"Like what?" He asked, his hands on his hips. "Maybe he used something like the lion's head?" Billy asked. "Or the ocular orb?"

"It's possible," she said.

Billy eyed her carefully, doubting that she was telling them everything. "And that's all there is to it? There's nothing else you can tell us about all of this?"

"I don't think so. I tried my best," she said. Ricky shook his head and turned away.

The buzzer rang. "Amy, you've got to help us get back," he said as they walked toward the school.

"Let's go in through the basement door," Amy said. "None of the kids use it, so nobody will ask about you."

The boys followed her into the basement and down the hall to the far stairs. Just below the stairs, she stopped them. "Wait until the halls are clear. It will be easier to sneak up to the vortex." After a few minutes, they heard footsteps coming down the stairs.

"Quick, hide in the washroom," Amy whispered. She led them into the girl's washroom. Ricky sighed and sat on the tiles. Billy paced nervously, but he was getting used to feeling uncomfortable. He stared at Amy. *Maybe he did have some ability that he didn't know about.* He looked at Ricky. *Why was he so mean to Amy? Is something happening that she hasn't told us about? Has he figured it out?*

Once the footsteps disappeared down the hall, Amy peeked around the wall. "We should be able to go upstairs now." She led them out of the washroom and up the stairs. In the main hall, the kids were in their classes, and the doors shut. When they neared the office, Mr. Dobbins swung around the corner in front of them. Amy stopped and waited for the boys to catch up.

"Be quiet," she whispered, "he doesn't approve of students out of class." Creeping forward, Billy could hear the rhythmic thump and tap of his footsteps and cane. His hands sweated. If Dobbins turned, he would see them.

Dobbins lifted the cane and rapped on a classroom door. The door opened, and Billy saw the brilliant white knob on the end of the dead black stick.

"Stop what you are doing right now!" Dobbins shouted. The voice sent chills up Billy's spine. Dobbins turned his head, and Billy gasped. His legs gave way, and he slumped to the floor.

81

The face last night. He pushed Becky. The man in the window. It's Dobbins!

CHAPTER TWELVE

Halloween

When he came around, Billy found himself upstairs. His hands shook, and his heart thumped like a hammer in his throat.

"What's the matter?" Amy asked, letting go of the gym door handle.

"It's him, Amy—Dobbins," he said, his voice breaking.

"What? What are you talking about?" she asked, leaning over him.

"Are you okay?" Ricky's face showed concern.

Billy gasped for air."Dobbins is the evil spirit. I looked in the doorway when we passed." He blurted it out. "The cane that Dobbins has is the lion's head." He rocked back and forth. "He's the evil spirit in our time."

"Are you sure?" Ricky asked.

"But he's the principal," Amy said, shaking her head. "He wouldn't hurt kids. He takes care of them."

Billy faced her and grabbed her shoulders. "I saw his face."

Her eyes flashed. "It can't be. He's the headmaster."

He squeezed her arms. "I heard his voice. You heard it as well as I did."

"I just don't bel—"

"It's the same face, the same voice as last night. He's the evil spirit!"

A door slammed down the hall. "Let's get out of the hallway." Ricky opened the gym door behind them.

They walked into the gym. "But why would he take the boys?" Amy asked.

The boys exchanged a look and then shook their heads. "Maybe he's making them do bad things," Ricky said.

She frowned. "Like what?"

He stared into her eyes. "You know. He's controlling them."

She shook her head. "I don't think so."

Billy put his hand on her shoulder. "He could use magic to control them."

"Making them his slaves," Ricky added.

"Slaves?" she shuddered and backed away. "What do you mean?"

Billy stepped forward. "Using magic to make them do what he wants."

"That sounds awful." She grabbed Billy by the arm. "We have to find them."

"I know. We will." He spoke as if he was talking to his sister.

"But we have to stop Dobbins, too," Ricky said.

Billy glanced from Ricky to Amy. "We have to do both."

"Okay," she said.

"But right now," Ricky said, "we need to get back to our time before we're missed."

"Oh, right." Amy removed the ocular orb from her pocket. "I still can't believe it's Dobbins."

"It's him, all right," Billy said, as he tried to get his head around what they needed to do.

"Are you certain?" she asked. "Believe me, it's him."

It was still recess when they arrived back in their own time and looked for the lion's head. After a little searching, Billy picked it up from under the piano.

"It's the same as what was on his cane. I'm sure of it," he said.

"Let me see." Amy studied it carefully. "You're right. It looks exactly like Dobbins's cane. What was that word you said?" "*Panthera Leo*. It means lion in Latin."

The Leo glowed. "It feels warm," she said. "*Panthera Leo*." The Leo glowed brighter. "It's hot!" She jerked her hand away and dropped it.

"Don't say it again," Ricky warned. "You'll make us go back in time."

"Don't worry, I won't." She shielded her eyes from the bright light. They watched as the light from the lion's head faded. Billy picked the Leo up and put it into his jacket pocket just as the recess bell rang. He and Ricky said goodbye to Amy as she pulled out the ocular orb, and they headed back to class.

--*-*-*

At the end of the day, Billy pushed his way into the crowded cloakroom. Kids chattered, laughed, and bumped each other as they claimed their belongings.

"Hey, Billy," Jonathon said from behind him. "You and Ricky going out as aliens again?"

"No, a wizard this year," replied Billy. He squeezed between two groups of girls, feeling a bit like a sardine in an overcrowded can.

"I'm going as Thor."

"Cool, maybe I'll see you around."

"Yeah, you, too."

Billy balanced his books with one hand and yanked his jacket off the hook with the other. He shoved his left hand into one sleeve and leaned forward to drop his books into his open backpack.

"Watch it," one of the girls said, jostling him and throwing him off balance. As his shoulder bumped the shelf, he grabbed the hook, swung his body around, and exclaimed when the lion's head flew from his pocket and landed with a thump somewhere on the floor. He searched around, but just as he reached for it, someone kicked it away, and it rolled out of the cloakroom.

"Oh great." He stood, threw his backpack over one shoulder, and pushed through the scrambling mass of kids, eyes following the Leo as it rolled.

"What's this?" said Andrew, stooping and picking it up as it stopped at his feet. "Cool."

"Andrew, that's mine," he said, thrusting his hand forward.

Andrew rolled it around in his hand. "I don't see your name on it."

"Come on, man, it fell out of my coat pocket."

Andrew pulled it away. "Prove it," he said with a grin.

"Andrew, give it back." Billy raised his voice.

"Is there a problem?" Mr. Moore asked from the doorway.

Andrew quickly shoved the Leo into his coat pocket. "No, sir." He winked at Billy and headed out the door.

Billy fumed, but said nothing. *I have to get that back somehow.* He zipped up his jacket and stuffed his belongings into his backpack. "Yeah, no problem, sir," he said as he passed. "Come on, Ricky, we're late."

"Late for what?" Ricky asked when they were outside. "And what was all that about, anyway?"

"The lion's head fell out of my pocket, and Andrew picked it up. He won't give it back. And I didn't want to explain it to Mr. Moore."

"Right," said Ricky. "Let him play with it. Maybe he'll send himself into oblivion."

"But we might need it against Dobbins."

"All magic does is get you into trouble."

"But what if Dobbins uses it through Andrew?"

"Oh, I hadn't thought of that. Anyway, let's not worry about it tonight. It's Halloween."

--*-*-*

"Ah, Mom, do I have to?" Billy said as he struggled with his wizard costume.

"She's your sister, and yes, you have to take her with you." His mom helped Sarah with her witch hat.

"Ah, Mom—"

"Stop it now." She frowned at him with one of those looks only moms could give, and Billy gave up.

"Oh, all right," he said, waving his wand around, wishing he could make his sister disappear.

The doorbell rang, and Sarah ran to answer it. A moment later, Ricky followed her into the kitchen, decked out as a mad magician, complete with a staff and cape.

"Wow. Look at you," Mrs. MacLean said as she smiled at him. Then she quickly turned to Billy. "Now, don't forget. No later than eight o'clock. It's a school night."

"Yes, Mom, we know," he and Sarah chorused as they exchanged a look and smiled.

"And don't go far. There's no telling what weird people go out on Halloween. If it's not wrapped, don't take it, and mind your sister."

"Yes, Mom." Billy rolled his eyes at Ricky.

"And have fun," she said, waving from the door. "What a worry wart," he said. Ricky snickered.

They walked through the thick fog. The street lamps looked like lighthouse beacons, and the house lights blurred in the distance. There was the after-smell of fireworks from the empty lot where the neighbor had let them off earlier. They jumped as fireworks ignited around them.

"I thought firecrackers were banned," Sarah said as she caught up to her brother.

"They are, but you can still get them if you know how," Ricky said. They approached the first house. Sarah shivered when they passed a hanging skeleton rattling in the wind. Billy rang the doorbell, which sounded more like a foghorn than a bell. The door creaked open, but nobody was there.

"Argh! Argh!" a pirate hoisting a rubber sword jumped out at them. Billy jumped back, and Sarah screamed. "Gotcha, me hardies. Argh, argh," the pirate said.

"Trick-or-treat!" the kids yelled.

"Ya want some o' me loot, do yar?"

"Yes, please," Sarah said as the pirate reached into a bowl and dropped handfuls of candy into their bags. "Thank you."

"A vast, ya swabs," he said when they turned, dodged the swinging skeleton, and dashed down the walk.

After trick or treating for five streets, Sarah stopped and complained that her bag was too heavy. "If you want the candy, you have to carry it," Billy said.

"Yeah, come on, Sarah, just a few more streets, okay?" Ricky asked.

Sarah dropped her bag with a thump. "But I'm tired," she said.

Billy groaned. "Just try."

"It's too heavy," she whined, almost falling over as she hoisted it over her shoulder and followed them onto the next street. They looked down the narrow roadway. One street lamp lit their way like a match in a dark room. The swirling fog was so thick they could barely see the one or two houses ahead. The acrid smell of fireworks was fresh in the air, and the wind blew swirls of dead leaves across their path. They walked to the street lamp.

Sarah dropped her bag. "It's too heavy," she said. "And this street is creepy."

"Stop complaining, Sarah. It's just Halloween." Billy dropped his bag. "And it's supposed to be scary."

"But I don't want to go any farther." She pulled her witch hat off and wiped her hair out of her eyes.

Billy sighed and glanced at his watch before gazing down the dark street. "What do you think, Ricky? Should we head back?"

Ricky watched the house lights flicker. "I don't mind, Billy."

"Okay, Sarah. If you're that tired, I guess we'll just have to go home, but you can't get any more candy then." He tried to sound disappointed.

She sighed. "I guess I'm not that tired." She picked up her bag.

"All right then," Billy said as he and Ricky hoisted their bags. "One more street."

Scree-eech! Scree-eech! Two loud rockets flew past them, barely missing their heads. Sarah screamed and dropped her bag. The boys stopped and gazed after the smoky missiles.

"What the heck," Billy said.

"Someone's shooting fireworks at us," Ricky said, squinting into the dark.

"I'm scared!" Sarah howled, grabbing onto her brother.

"It's okay," he said, putting his arm around her while his eyes darted around. "Let's just go home."

"You're not going anywhere." A ragged, poorly as sembled wizard appeared out of the swirling fog. "Stay put!" he ordered.

Billy recognized the voice. "Andrew?" Before he could react, three tall kids stepped in front of them.

One, in a devil's mask, held a rocket in one hand and a glowing match in the other. "Maybe another blast?" he said, glancing at the scruffy wizard. A zombie stood on one side of him and a vampire on the other.

"Maybe we should see what goodies they've brought us first," Andrew said.

"No way, Andrew." Ricky raised his staff up over his head.

"Pretty brave for a little shit," the vampire said, lunging at Ricky, who swung the staff, but the boy grabbed it and yanked it from his grip. Ricky rushed him only to have the vampire shove it hard into his stomach, bowling him over.

"Leave us alone!" Sarah shouted at them.

Billy pushed her away. "Go home!" he shouted.

She stepped back a few paces and clutched her bag. "Are you going to save him?" Andrew asked her as the boys laughed.

"Sarah. Go home." She just stepped a little further away.

"And how about you, Wiz?" continued the ragged wizard. "Or should I say, Billy? Are you going to stop us with a spell?"

Billy, eyes wide, hands clenched, frowned at Andrew. "I could if you didn't have your goons with you," he said. His heart pounded as he looked at Ricky writhing on the ground. *What could he do?*

"Hear that, guys? He called you goons," Andrew said. The zombie rushed forward, but Billy swung his bag and knocked him to the side. The zombie grabbed Billy by his cape, whirled him around and let go, diving onto Billy as he landed with a thump on the wet lawn.

They rolled around, kicking and pounding each other. Sarah screamed as the vampire grabbed her bag, and the devil mask shot a rocket at Ricky, who dodged it and stood up.

"Leave us alone!" Sarah shrieked. She jumped at the vampire, but he threw her off, and she landed with a thud on the sidewalk, her candy flying everywhere. Billy scrambled out from under his attacker and back to his feet. He and Ricky charged the vampire and knocked him over. The zombie threw Ricky off the vampire, but Billy hung on and managed to bloody the blood sucker's nose before the zombie kicked at his groin, narrowly missing and smashing the inside of Billy's thigh with his boot. He buckled from the pain and fell. Ricky leaped at the older boys, but they spun him around, and the devil kneed him in the stomach. He coughed and fell in a heap on the pavement.

"Why don't you use your magic wand?" Andrew said, watching from a safe distance. "Or how about this lion's head?" He pulled it from his coat pocket.

"Ricky. *Panthera Leo*," Billy snapped. The lion's head glowed in Andrew's hand.

"*Panthera Leo!*" Relief washed over Billy as Ricky's voice joined his in the shout.

The Leo blazed white hot in Andrew's hand. He yelped in pain, dropped it on the ground, and backed away, shielding his eyes. As the white, blinding light pierced the dark, Billy raised his arm over his face and shouted, "Cover your eyes, Sarah!" Shafts of light eerily illuminated the houses, trees, and cars, like rays from an alien spaceship.

"Let's get out of here," Andrew said as he turned and ran. The older boys dropped the bags and ran after him. The light from the lion's head slowly dissipated as their footsteps echoed into the night.

CHAPTER THIRTEEN

Ricky

"Are they gone?" Sarah rubbed her eyes, and refilled her candy bag.

"Yes, Sarah. You're safe now," Billy said.

"What was that?" she asked.

"That's the magic of the lion's head." Billy picked it up. It was still warm.

"Yeah, thank goodness we knew how to do it," Ricky said as he stuffed the spilled candy back into their bags.

"Let's go home," Billy said. "And Sarah, you can't say anything to Mom, okay?"

"Why? We should tell the police about those boys, shouldn't we?"

"Not this time. Besides, how are we going to explain the lion's head?"

"But they hurt you," Sarah argued as they crossed the street.

"I'm all right. Look, I'll give you some of my candy if you don't tell, okay?"

"Okay, but I want the chocolate bars."

"How about ten of them?"

"Okay, but you have to give me ten sour gums, too, then."

"Oh, all right, but you gotta promise you won't tell."

"Don't worry, I won't." Sarah smiled at her big brother. "But you have to tell me about that lion's head."

"Uh-huh," he said, winking at Ricky.

"I would have kept it secret without the chocolate bars," she said.

"I know," Billy replied with a grin. Soon they were back on their own street.

When they arrived home, they handed their bags over to Billy's mom for inspection and then collapsed in the living room.

"Mom, can we watch a movie?" Billy called.

"Yes, but not a long one. It's a school night." He winced as he hobbled over to the cabinet and scanned the titles.

"How about Halloween 3?" he asked.

"Sounds good," Ricky said. Sarah nodded her head, and Billy put it in the Blu-ray player.

"Can we have some candy, Mom?" Sarah asked.

"Yes, but not too much," Mrs. MacLean answered.

The kids rushed into the kitchen to choose their goodies.

"Billy, what's wrong with your leg?" she asked as he limped into the kitchen.

His hand on his bag, he hesitated as his mother caught his eye. "Nothing, Mom, I just tripped over the sidewalk and scraped it." He dropped his gaze and rooted through his candy, picking out a Coffee Crisp. "I'll be okay." Sarah and Ricky watched warily when she looked him up and down.

"Are you bleeding? Do you need a bandage?"

"No, I'm fine. It's just bruised."

"Okay," she said, sipping her tea, one eyebrow raised. Her eyes followed him when the kids walked back to the living room.

--*-*-*

Mrs. MacLean poked her head into the room as the credits started to roll. "Sarah, you get ready and washed up first." Sarah hopped off the couch and rustled out of the room in her witch costume.

Billy's mom eyed him again as he got up off the chair and limped over to the TV. "Are you sure you're okay?" she asked.

"Yeah, I'm fine. Come on, Ricky." Billy put the movie away. "I'll have you a war game on the computer while we wait for Sarah to get ready for bed." He glanced back to see his mom biting her lip and shaking her head before she sat down and changed the channel.

"Not long, boys. Lights out in half an hour," she called as they entered Billy's room.

"I'm glad you stayed over, Ricky. We've got to figure out what we're going to do next." Billy pulled the Leo from his pocket, flopped onto his bed, and gazed into the dark outside his window.

"At least we've got the lion's head back." Ricky glanced around the room. "Cool poster, dude. When did you get that?" He pointed to a large colorful poster above Billy's bed, pinned to the ceiling. It was a red and black dragon attacking a medieval castle with a moat around it.

"Last week. Dad brought it back from his trip to L.A. Here, catch." He tossed the Leo to Ricky, who was leaning against the dresser.

"Careful, man," Ricky said as he caught the lion's head. "What are we going to do with this thing?"

"You know, I've been thinking about that. Did you notice that when we both said the 'P' word," Billy replied, not wanting to set it off, "that it was more powerful?"

Ricky frowned. "What do you mean?"

"Like tonight. We both said the word, and it burst brighter than it has ever been. I think we are stronger when we are together. That's why Dobbins wants to destroy us."

"What?"

"Don't you see? Together we can defeat him."

"Whoa, mate. I don't know if I'd jump to that conclusion. We might be stronger, but defeat him? How?"

"By using the Leo." Billy waved his Harry Potter wand over his head. "And if we have Amy join us, we'll be invincible." He swished left and right, fighting an imaginary Dobbins.

"Easy, man. This isn't a Harry Potter movie. We have a lot of figuring out to do before we even think about going after him."

"I know, Ricky, but we did it. We beat Andrew. Look how we took care of him and his buddies."

"Kids are one thing, Billy. Evil spirits are another."

"Billy, Ricky! Sarah's out of the washroom! Get ready for bed!" Mom yelled from the living room.

"Okay!" Billy answered as he bounced off the bed. He took the Leo from Ricky and shoved it into his dresser drawer.

--*-*-*

As they sat on the front steps of the school the next morning, Billy yawned and watched the wind whip the leaves into piles against the trees. He drew in a deep breath, stretched, and rubbed his eyes. He and Ricky had spent half the night talking about magic, Amy, and Dobbins, but he still did not know how to stop the evil headmaster. He shivered and zipped his jacket up. The crows cawed under the grey clouds above, and kids played tag and munched on candies.

"Billy, Ricky, how was your Halloween?" Jonathon called as he came up the path swigging a can of soda. "Europ!" he belched and laughed.

Billy laughed. "Rude, dude," Ricky said.

"It was kind of quiet," Billy said, raising his brows toward Ricky.

"Not mine," Jonathon said. "We went trick-or-treating and then to the bonfire behind the arena, and some kid threw fireworks into it and lit a shed on fire."

"Whoa," Billy said.

"Yeah, and a fire truck came and put it out."

"Cool," Ricky said. "Anybody get hurt?"

"Nah, it was just an old broken-down building on that empty lot. You know, where they're going to put the new pool." The bell rang, and the kids ran for the door. Ms. Fenton clanged the old school bell and hollered at the screaming mob to slow down.

After last night's excitement, the day dragged. Even recess and lunch were slow and boring. Billy's thigh throbbed as he hobbled around the playground. *What should we do next? How are we going to stop Dobbins?* He was about to ask Ricky a question when he remembered that Dobbins could hear them. It would have to wait.

--*-*-*

Stephen, who sat in front of Ricky, barfed all over the floor. The kids groaned and wailed as they escaped to the cloakroom. Mr. Moore rang the janitor but got no answer. "Ricky, will you run down to the boiler room and get the janitor, please? We're going to need a mop and bucket right away."

"Yes, sir," Ricky replied. "Meet you outside," he said to Billy. He headed down the hall, and Billy went out the door. *At least this boring day is over.* He looked around the playground. *Andrew isn't here today.* Billy smiled. *He's probably still scared.* Billy forgot about him when Jonathon called to him. He waved and limped over to join a few others setting up a soccer game, taking goal because of his sore leg.

After what seemed like hours, Jonathon's mom bellowed at him from across the field, and the game broke up.

That's odd. Where's Ricky? Billy hustled back to the classroom, but it was silent and empty, smelling of disinfectant. Ricky's coat and backpack hung on his hook. A thread of alarm wormed its way up his back. *Why is his stuff still here?* He hurried from the room, heading for the basement stairs. Near the boiler room, a cold chill surrounded him. *I don't like this.*

He patted the Leo in his pocket. Ice bit into his fingers when he touched the doorknob. He snatched his hand away and glanced down the hall, but there was nothing else to do. He reached out slowly and turned the knob as the bone-chilling cold burned his hand. A swirl of arctic air blew through him like a slash of icicles, but he yanked it open. He grabbed the handrail and rode the winter blast until it subsided, and silence surrounded him like a tomb. *What was that?* He flicked the overhead light on. Nothing and no one showed themselves. *Is someone here?* The hair on the back of his neck pricked as he took a halting breath. Slowly, he walked down the stairs to the boiler room. Even the furnace was quiet. At the bottom, he peered into the dark recesses of the room but could see nothing.

"Ricky?" he whispered, afraid to disturb whatever was there.

No answer.

He cleared his throat. "Ricky, are you here?" Nothing. He searched among the boxes and mops, shelves of towels and paper, but Ricky wasn't anywhere. "I wonder what happened to him."

"That's a good question," someone said from the doorway. Billy screeched and whirled around to see the custodian standing on the steps.

"Who are you looking for?" the janitor said, scratching his head.

"Ricky Stevens. He was sent to get you."

"Really?" The grey-haired man screwed up his face. "When?"

"Right after school," Billy replied, feeling a little uncomfortable. "I guess he went home."

"Probably—you'd better head home, too. It's getting late."

"I will," he said, rushing up the stairs and out into the hall. *Where is Ricky?* Billy's breath caught in his throat, and a cold sweat moistened his skin. The hall was empty. No footsteps sounded, no voices carried from the office or any of the classrooms. He shivered and glanced around, starting to panic.

CHAPTER FOURTEEN

The Small Room

Billy flew down the hall and up the stairs to the classroom. Ricky's coat and backpack still hung on their hook. *Dobbins has him.* He grabbed Ricky's stuff.

"Mrs. Niles, Ricky's missing," he said, tossing Ricky's things on the table in front of the secretary's desk.

"What do you mean, missing?" She spat the words out, scowling at him from over her glasses as though he had disturbed a very important chore.

"I can't find him anywhere, and his coat and backpack are still here."

"Maybe he just forgot to take them home." She tapped her pen on the desk. "It wouldn't be the first time. Kids leave their things everywhere."

He dropped his backpack on the floor. "He wouldn't leave them here. I know it."

The secretary dropped her pen, stared at him and sighed from deep within her soul. "All right, all right," she said, reaching for the phone. "Let me call his house and see if he's there, okay?"

Billy wrung his hands and paced about the room as she dialed. He tugged the Leo from his pocket and tossed it into the air. "*Panthera, panthera, panthera,*" he muttered. When he caught it, it was warm and had turned dark. Murky clouds swirled on its surface. *Did I do that?*

"Sit down," the secretary snapped.

Billy slid into the chair by the table, the Leo still warm in his hand. "*Panthera, panthera, panthera,*" he whispered. Clouds of grey and black swirled again. He stared at it. *Can I do more?*

Bored, he tapped his fingernails on the tabletop until Mrs. Niles glared. He stuffed the Leo back into his pocket and smiled. Finally, the secretary put the receiver back on its cradle and looked hard at Billy. "There's no answer. Maybe he went out with his mom or dad."

"I don't think so. He—"

"I'm sure he's okay." Mrs. Niles looked over her glasses. "He probably had a doctor's appointment or something." Billy frowned and grabbed his backpack. "It'll be okay," she repeated as he left the office. *No, it won't.*

Outside, he gazed up at the school. "No one else knows Ricky is in trouble. Nobody is listening to me," he muttered.

--*-*-*

Billy lay on his bed staring at the dragon on his ceiling. *Ricky has been missing for two hours, and still no word. Where would Dobbins take him?* He drew the lion's head out of his pocket and tossed it in the air. *What if he's done something horrible to him?* After a few tosses, he sat up and focused on it. What else can I do with this? "*Panthera, panthera, panthera,*" he whispered. The lion's head warmed in his hand. Nothing else happened. "*Panthera, panthera, panthera,*" he repeated. Clouds swirled across its surface as they had in the office.

"What should I try?" He looked around his room at the mess on the floor. "Tidy my room." The black and grey sat there. So did his clothes, books, and video games. Billy concentrated. "*Panthera, panthera, panthera,*" he barked. At first, it swirled black and grey, then it turned crystal clear. Billy focused with all of his might. "Tidy my room!" The clear ball did nothing.

"Ah." He grimaced and dropped the Leo on the bed. "Why can't I do this?" He lay back and stared at the dragon for a while. *What would Amy do?*

"I know. I need to use a spell." He hopped off the bed and grabbed his laptop. "Spells. Spells. Where do I find spells? Ah, here we go, 'Magic Spells for Everyday Use.'" He clicked through several pages on magic until he found one that offered what he was looking for. "How to invoke simple tasks."

Knock! Knock! "Billy, are you okay?" His mom called from the hallway. In a panic, Billy minimized the screen and popped the Leo into his desk drawer.

"Yes, Mom." The door opened, and Mrs. MacLean entered. She placed his dinner down on his night table and sat on his bed. "I brought your dinner, and I want you to try and eat some of it, okay?"

"Yeah," he answered.

She reached forward and touched his forehead.

He pulled his head away. "I'm okay, just worried about Ricky."

"I understand. It's hard when you don't know where he is, but I'm sure he's all right. There's probably a logical explanation for his books and coat. Try to relax, okay?"

"Uh-huh," he said, nodding his head.

She gave him a smile and stood up. "Eat it up before it gets cold. I'll come back for the plate in a bit."

He sighed when she left the room. "That was close," he muttered as he retrieved the lion's head from the drawer. He picked up his laptop. "Where was I?" he whispered, clicking the mouse. "That one looks good—'a cleaning spell'." He rubbed the Leo. "*Panthera, panthera, panthera.*" The lion's head warmed up again. "*Panthera, panthera, panthera,*" he repeated as he gazed into it. The Leo changed from white and black to crystal. The phone in the hall rang. Billy ignored it, narrowed his gaze, and focused. "*Cella redige,*" he said. He looked hopefully around his room, but it didn't tidy itself. He stared hard at the Leo. "*Cella redige—*"

"Billy," his mom called from the hallway. "Ricky's dad is on the phone."

"Oh, crap," Billy muttered. "Coming." Dropping the Leo, he slipped into the hall before she could get to the door.

"Hello?"

"Hello, Billy?" Ricky's dad asked.

"Yes, sir?"

"Do you know where Ricky is?" He sounded more like a cop than the way he usually did.

Billy closed his eyes as hope and fear rushed through him, making him feel lightheaded. Help at last! He hesitated. *What could he say, "Yeah, but I can't tell you?" Wouldn't that go over well?* "No, I don't, sir." *You gotta believe me.*

"Did you see him after school?"

Billy gulped as his guilt rose, trapping his words in his throat. Ricky was gone, but he couldn't tell Sergeant Stevens about Dobbins. Ricky's dad would never believe it.

"Yes, I saw him before he went to get the janitor."

"Why did he have to do that?"

"Because, Stephen barfed all over the place."

"Oh, too much Halloween candy, I bet."

Billy forced a laugh. "Yeah, I guess so."

"Did you see him after that?" Sergeant Stevens's cop voice returned.

"No, that's when he disappeared." His hopes flared again. *Please believe me.*

"What do you mean he disappeared?" The policeman's biting tone cut the background hiss of the line.

Billy struggled with his words. *How could he convince Ricky's dad without sounding ridiculous?* "I mean, he didn't come back."

"And what did you do?" Sergeant Stevens led him through the events of the afternoon, from playing soccer while waiting for Ricky, to his trip to the office.

"And then Mom called, and I had to come home," Billy finished. *And you've got to find him.*

Ricky's dad was quiet for a moment. "Did he say what he was going to do after school?"

He heard the doubt in Sergeant Stevens' voice. He gripped the phone tightly. *Why doesn't he believe me? I told him the truth.* "No, sir."

"Really?" the policeman said. "And you boys didn't have anything planned?"

Billy's frustration heated him like a fever. He strangled the phone in his hands. *How can I make him believe me?* "No, sir," he replied.

"Are you sure, Billy?" The voice pushed for a different answer.

Hope drained out of Billy, leaving him empty and tired. He didn't know what else to say. "Yes, sir."

Ricky's dad sighed and cleared his throat. "Did he seem upset at all?"

"No, he was fine today. Mr. Stevens, if he were going to run away or something, I'd have known. And why wouldn't he take his things with him?"

"Yes, that doesn't sound like Ricky, all right. And you're sure he didn't tell you he wanted to go somewhere after school?" There was a short pause, and Sergeant Stevens's voice came over the phone, clipped and sharp. "Because if he did, you need to tell me."

Billy gulped, as he tried to contain his frustration. "No, I would have remembered that, Mr. Stevens."

Ricky's dad sighed. "Okay, Billy," he said. The line buzzed for a moment. Neither Billy nor Ricky's dad spoke. *He's disappeared, and you need to try to find him.* "Sir, if he ran away, why would he leave his stuff behind?"

"I don't know. I'll check the school to make sure. One last time, son, he didn't mention anything to you, right?"

Billy thought for a moment. "He just said something about playing a new video game tonight. That's all."

"You're his best friend, Billy. How could you not know where he is?"

Billy gulped at the pain in his voice. "I don't know, Mr. Stevens, but if he'd said something, I'd tell you, honest I would."

"Think hard, Billy. He's my son. Where is he?" Billy desperately wanted to tell him about Dobbins, but he couldn't.

"I'm sorry, Mr. Stevens," he said, tears welling up in his eyes. "I really don't know where he is."

The line hummed as Ricky's dad was silent for several seconds. "All right, Billy, but if you hear from him, phone me right away, okay?"

Billy's heart began to pound. "Yup, I promise I will."

There was another long pause. Billy fidgeted and almost dropped the receiver. *I wish he would just believe me. If only I could tell him everything.*

"I'll talk to you soon," Sergeant Stevens said and hung up.

Billy held the receiver until the dial tone kicked in, and then he put it back on the cradle.

"Any word about Ricky?" his mom asked.

"No, Sergeant Stevens hasn't seen him either. And he asked me if Ricky was thinking about running away."

She frowned. "And was he?"

"Not as far as I know."

She stared at him, her hands on her hips. "Are you sure?" Billy's face burned as his anger spilled over. "I already told you. He disappeared at school this afternoon. I don't know what happened to him! Why doesn't anyone believe me?"

"William Arthur Maclean! Don't you raise your voice to me!"

Billy took a deep breath and chewed his lip before saying anything more."But I've already told you, Mom. Remember? When you called the school? I told you that he went to get the janitor and didn't come back." He threw his hands up in frustration. "Why won't you believe me?"

She reached for his hands. "Yes, you did, and I'm sorry if it sounds as if I don't believe you. I do. It's just that you're his best friend. He wouldn't do anything without telling you, would he?"

"That's just it," Billy said, sobbing. "He didn't tell me anything, Mom. That's why I think something happened to him."

"I understand," she said as she put her arms around him. "Don't worry. If anyone can find him, his dad can."

Billy cried and hugged her back. "I guess so." He sobbed into her neck. After a few minutes, she released him, and he felt her eyes on his back as he headed to his room.

He lay back on his bed and shut his eyes. *Did he run away? Why? Nothing special happened. At least he didn't say anything had.*

His stomach growled, so he sat up and ate mechanically. *Ricky would have said something if he was planning it. He would have given it away somehow, even if he didn't tell me. I would have known. He can't hide that stuff from me.* He shook his head and mopped up the rest of the mac and cheese. *Dobbins has him. It's the only answer.*

He stood up like a robot and took the empty plate to the kitchen, more worried than ever. *If he waited for the adults to help, Ricky would be lost forever. He had to do something. But what? How could he find Ricky and, once he'd found him, get him away from Dobbins?*

Back in his room, he turned the laptop on and grabbed the Leo. "*Panthera, panthera, panthera,*" he whispered. The lion's head warmed up and cleared right away. He looked for the words to the spell again. "*Cella redige,*" he whispered as he gazed into the orb. The crystal clouded over as a grey fog swirled inside the sphere. "*Cella redige!*" he commanded. The orb cleared, and Billy felt a wind on his face as books, games, and clothes swirled about his room, finding their rightful places. "Wow," Billy whispered. Grinning with delight, he stared, fascinated, as drawers opened and clothes jumped in; books hopped up onto shelves, and his video game collection not only put itself back on the shelf, but organized itself as well. "This is cool."

As the wind settled down and the sphere turned white again, he grabbed his laptop. "What else can I do? Maybe I can use it to help me find Ricky—wouldn't that be great?" He smiled as he surfed the Internet, feeling like a sorcerer's apprentice.

"This spell looks perfect. '*Ubi es, Ricky?*'" Billy set down the laptop and focused on the Leo. "*Panthera, panthera, panthera.*" The disk went clear in an instant. "*Ubi es, Ricky?*" The orb swirled for a second before a clear image appeared. He strained to see into the little ball. A room came into view, no larger than a closet. *Is it a room in the school? A hidden room?*

He stared at dark walls and a darker shadow against one wall. Slowly, the image cleared, and he made out arms and legs. An arm was raised, and a body lurched back and forth. "Ricky, is that you? Are you okay? Where are you?" The blurred figure lowered its head, still and silent. He watched in terror as the figure raised its head. Billy squeezed the Leo, his heart pounding. *It was Ricky!*

"Ricky, where are you?" No response. His eyes looked blank. Billy shook the orb in frustration. "Why can't you hear me?" As he willed a connection, the lion's head swirled again, and another space came into view with a small body lying on the floor. Billy jumped back and dropped the orb onto his bed. *What was that?*

He stared at it, terrified, as the murky clouds reformed and then cleared, leaving the ball its usual plain white. Disappointed, worried, and frustrated, his eyes stung, and he blinked back his tears. "I'm going to find you, buddy. Don't worry. I'm going to stop Dobbins." His breath hitched, and tears tracked down his cheeks.

After a few minutes, Billy wiped his eyes, picked up the Leo, now cool, and put it on top of his clothes. "I'm going to find you, Ricky. I'll go to the school, before anyone else is there, and rescue you, don't worry." He turned off his laptop, set his alarm for early in the morning, and got into bed. *I can't forget it in the morning.* When he closed his eyes, all he could see was Ricky's dead stare.

CHAPTER FIFTEEN

Derek

Between the howling wind and the driving rain, Billy was soaked by the time he entered the school grounds early the next morning. The faint lights around the building exposed the tall, rustic bricks of Lampson. He glanced at his watch as he huddled under a tree, wiping the water from his face. *Six forty-five. No wonder the roads were so quiet; all normal souls were still asleep.* Hopefully, his mom wouldn't phone the cops or anything after she read his note.

Gazing around the parking lot, he spied the janitor's white truck sitting where it was always parked. *Now how am I going to get in?* He stared at the big green garbage bin. *Maybe the janitor will open a door and bring out the trash.* A small step stool that the kids used to reach the top of the bin leaned against it. He sneaked over to the bin, grabbed the stool, and ran around back to his classroom.

"Aha!" He placed the stool under a small open window. There was enough gap to get his fingers under it. He climbed the steps, yanked the window open, and crawled over the sill, falling onto a few cardboard boxes stuffed with paper. He cringed and lay still, listening for the janitor, but all was quiet. The sparse light from the hallway allowed him to navigate the rows of desks.

Thump! He froze, focusing on the textbook he had knocked off a desk. His heart pounded. *Did anyone hear me?* Nobody came. The only sound was Murphy, the class gerbil, scurrying around his cage. In the hallway, he thrust his hand into his pocket and rubbed the lion's head. *But I don't know any good spells.*

"That won't stop me," he whispered, staring down the basement stairs. A few steps down, he heard footsteps coming up. He turned abruptly and dashed back up to the top, his heart in his throat, hands sweaty. Someone coughed. *Where can I hide?* He sprinted on tiptoes toward the open library door. Another cough by the office. Billy hid behind the librarian's desk and peered over it. A white form floated into the room. He gasped and pushed back against the desk. The hair on the back of his neck stood up, and his sweaty hands slid along the polished wood. The transparent shape solidified into a boy with blond hair and blue eyes. Billy recognized the blue cardigan with two gaping holes in it and black trousers. "W-who are you?"

"I'm Derek," the boy said.

"What are you doing here?"

"I'm always here. You haven't much time. Follow me."

Billy watched in fascination as the spirit floated back to the door. Exhaling, Billy pushed himself to his feet. "Why should I follow you?" he whispered.

The ghost floated back a few feet. "You want to find your friend, don't you?"

"You know where he is?"

"Yes." Derek floated toward the door. "But we have to be quick."

"Why?"

"Because Mr. Dobbins will be back soon."

Billy hesitated. *It could be a trap, but if I don't go and it's not...* "Okay," he said, following Derek into the hallway. He looked both ways. No janitor.

"This way," the boy said, beckoning him to the right. Billy gulped and followed. They slid down the staircase to the basement.

"Derek?" Billy stopped. The blond-haired boy turned around. "Where is Dobbins, and why doesn't he know what you're doing?"

"He's busy with the others."

"Others?" Billy rolled the Leo in his pocket.

"You know, the other boys."

"What other boys?"

"The ones he has taken."

"They're not all together then?"

"No, Ricky's in a special place. Come on. We have to hurry." Derek turned and flew forward. Billy paused to think. *I guess I don't have a choice if I want to help Ricky—if he really is taking me to him.* He pushed down his fear and followed.

A chill struck his face as he approached the boiler room door. A shiver crawled down his back, and his heart pounded. *"Panthera Leo,"* he whispered, and the glowing lion's head warmed his hand and gave him reassurance.

He stared at Derek's flashing blue eyes. "In here," he said, sliding through the boiler room door. Billy gulped, took a deep breath, and opened the door.

"Ignus draconi!" A blast of red light struck his chest like a lightning bolt. He screamed and fell to the ground, pain shooting through his body like fire.

Dobbins, draped in a black robe, floated before him, his white bony fingers aiming a black cane at Billy. The evil yellow eyes flashed in the gaunt face.

"Dolorem!" Dobbins yelled. Billy rolled, but not far enough, and another fiery bolt crackled, hitting him in the gut.

Billy shrieked and writhed on the floor. Fighting through the pain, he yanked the Leo from his pocket. *"Panthera Leo!"* he yelled, aiming the white light at Dobbins. It clashed with the red, forming a brilliant arc above them, hissing and shearing off sparks like a Tesla coil, smashing the ceiling and walls. Billy focused his energy and threw a burst of light forward, matching Dobbins.

"You're not strong enough, boy!" Dobbins snarled, forcing the sizzling glare toward Billy.

His heart thumping, he stared in terror as the red streak snapped and sparked closer and closer to the Leo. Concentrating with all of his might, he held his ground. *"Panthera Leo!"* he screamed, boosting the white bolt. The Leo's eyes glowed as the red fire crept back toward Dobbins.

"You don't know how to use magic!" Dobbins flicked his fingers, sending the fiery bolt forward again.

Sweating, his hands shaking, Billy held fast to the Leo. *"Leo claresco,"* he shouted. The Leo's light burst brighter. The red light stopped again.

"You will lose!" Dobbins yelled, his yellow eyes penetrating. "*Ignus draconi!*" he screamed. The red glow crept closer, reaching the lion's head and inching toward his fingers.

"No, I won't!" Billy cried. "*Leo claresco!*" he shouted, impelling the Leo, driving the snapping red sparks back.

The lights glowed and crackled as the two parried and lunged. Billy rallied each time Dobbins forced him into a corner. The flashes lit the whole boiler room like fireworks. Finally, Billy fell to his knees, his head throbbing with exhaustion.

Dobbins towered over him. "Let it go, boy, and I will stop your pain." Billy took a deep breath and hung on. The red-forked beam drew closer to the Leo, snapping and snarling like a dragon.

"No." Billy rose to his feet. "*Leo conteret eum!*" The quick strike sent the white glare snapping toward a stunned Dobbins.

He quickly countered. "*Leo sistenda.*" The white light stopped its advance. "I will do to you what I've done to Ricky," Dobbins warned.

Billy ignored him. His head pounded, and his chest heaved with strain. The red beam crackled and slithered closer. His whole being ached. *What can I do? Amy, I need your strength.*

Dobbins smiled.

The fiery bolt hissed and flashed just inches away from the Leo's eyes and Billy's fingers. He felt the burning heat as he lost focus, his power faltering. *It can't end here. A spell? Or?*

"*Ego vos perficiam—*"

"*Panthera Leo, Panthera Leo, Panthera Leo!*" Billy screamed with his last ounce of strength.

CHAPTER SIXTEEN

Tommy

Billy screamed in pain as he disappeared into the dark. *Thud!* He slammed into the floor underneath him, but the darkness still surrounded him. He turned toward the heat on his left. A line of light traced the outline of a door. *Is the boiler room on the other side?* He shook himself and rose to his feet. The room spun, and he leaned against the wall, weak and shivering. A musty, cave-like smell assaulted him as he groped his way along the walls. He tripped a switch, and a soft light from a hanging bulb flashed on, revealing another doorway at the far end of the passage. He was in some kind of hallway between two rooms.

He tried to decide which door to open when a voice startled him. "Who are you?"

Billy staggered back as a faint image of a boy floated in front of him. It wasn't Derek. This kid appeared to be a little younger than Derek. He wore a white shirt, a bowtie, and dark trousers.

"Who are you, and where am I?" Billy asked.

The spirit paused for a moment, eyeing him up and down. "I'm Tommy."

Maybe he can help me. "Where am I?"

"This is a storage room," Tommy said, floating about.

He pointed at the door behind the spirit. "What's in there?"

"Come, and I'll show you," the spirit answered, floating toward the door.

"Hold on," Billy said. "I followed a ghost before, and I was nearly killed."

"Who?"

"His name was Derek, and he tricked me."

"Derek? He's one of us."

"What do you mean, 'one of you?'"

"Come, and I'll show you," Tommy repeated. "You're one of Dobbins's boys. I'm not going to follow you." He turned toward the heat behind him.

Tommy slid in front of him. "Wait, I want to help you."

"Sure, just like Derek, who led me into a trap. Why should I believe you?"

"Because I want to show you what Mr. Dobbins has done. I want him stopped before he hurts anyone else."

Billy eyed the hazy boy for a moment. *Maybe he's telling the truth.* "Can you tell me where Dobbins is right now?"

"Yes." Tommy looked past Billy for a moment. "He's in his office."

Should I believe him? "And who knows about this room?"

"I don't know, but it's locked, and he has the key."

"And where does that door lead?" Billy turned around.

"Let me show you." Tommy flew over to it. A lump formed in Billy's throat. *Should I trust him? What if it's another trap? Then again, I can't stay here.*

"Okay," he said, clutching the doorknob. The ghost slipped through the door. Billy took a deep breath, afraid to open it. *What if Dobbins is on the other side? Should I...* He gulped and turned it. Cold air washed over his face, and static electricity jolted his fingers as if someone had touched him after charging their nylon socks on a carpet. He jumped back against the wall.

"What is that?" he said, eyeing a crackling cloud in the middle of the room.

"That's what keeps us here," Tommy whispered, hovering over three clothed lumps lying on the floor. Billy's heart thumped, and his stomach rolled. The light from the corridor behind illuminated three still faces. He struggled forward.

"That's us," Tommy said. Billy gulped and blinked. Three boys stared back with frozen eyes, lifeless as dolls. One was Derek, and one was Tommy. The third he did not recognize. They were as still as death.

"What happened to you?" Billy asked, backing up and bracing himself against the wall, his knees wobbling, heart pounding.

"Mr. Dobbins put a spell on us."

"That's horrible, but why?"

"So he can control us."

Billy's stomach churned as he scrambled back into the passageway. "I can't stay here," he mumbled, clawing along the walls until his hands encountered a doorknob. His stomach lurched, and his hands shook. He cranked it open and fell through, clinging to the knob for balance. The heat struck his face and he stumbled across the room, landing on the floor. He pushed himself to a sitting position, shaking from head to toe, and sat gazing through the passageway behind him. *Those are bodies, aren't they?* The room swam in front of him, and he dropped his head to his knees. The reality of it engulfed him. He jerked his head up to gasp in a lungful of hot, clean air and shot his legs out straight in front of him.

"That's what happened to us, Billy." Tommy floated above him. "He keeps us there." Tears streamed down Billy's face. He stared blankly, rubbing his sweaty hands on his jeans and shivering. Tommy floated closer and leaned toward him. "Mr. Dobbins did this."

Billy crawled forward and pushed the door to the passageway shut, then slid back against the wall. "Tom my," he gasped, the words catching in his throat. "H- how...how many?"

"Three of us so far. You have to help us."

Billy shuddered and took deep breaths as he tried to compose himself. He wiped the sweat from his forehead and took in the toilet paper boxes, cleaning supplies, and the janitor's desk in the adjacent room.

"You have to help us, Billy."

He fought the mental images of three cold bodies and focused on Tommy. "How?"

"You have to stop Mr. Dobbins."

As the horror flooded over him, he shivered and pushed it away, trying to focus on the conversation. "Why did Dobbins do this?"

"He's evil. He uses our energy, making himself more powerful to do his horrible spells and capture more souls."

111

Billy trembled. "How does he do that?" Tommy looked sad. "He's put a spell on us."

Billy stiffened. *Three of us so far*. He sucked in his breath. The meaning of Tommy's words sank in. "Oh, my God—Ricky's next!"

"Who's Ricky?"

Billy shook his head. "Never mind," he said, struggling to his feet. "I've got to find Amy."

"Who's she?" Tommy floated beside the furnace.

"Someone who can help." He staggered up the steps, yanked open the door, and slipped out into the hall. He paused and leaned against the wall, catching his breath while revisiting Dobbins's terrible secret. Climbing the basement stairs, he peeked over the railing at the top. Good, it was deserted. He glanced at the office clock. Eight ten. He had time to find her before the bell rang. Dashing to the right, he opened the door and stepped outside. He braced himself against the wall, letting the cool air wash over him as he caught his breath before he hurried around the school, scanning the grounds for Amy.

Finally, he spied her standing beside an oak tree. "Amy," he called, running to her.

"Billy, what are you doing here?" she asked, her eyes round.

"I found three bodies, and Ricky needs our help before Dobbins—"

She grabbed his arm. "What? Slow down; you're not making sense."

"But we've got to hurry. To save Ricky."

She pulled him to the basement door. "Calm down, Billy."

"There's no time, Amy. Dobbins is going to kill him."

She ignored him, yanked the door open, and shoved him through. "Now," she whispered. "Tell me what's going on."

Out of breath, he gasped. "Dobbins has Ricky... found the bodies... the lost boys."

"You found bodies?" She stared at him, eyes wide. "W-what do you mean?" She stopped, a look of terror dawning on her face.

"The bodies of the lost boys." He stared back. "At least, they sure looked dead. Dobbins must have killed them."

"Oh, my God!" Tears welled up in her eyes. "But why?"

"He's using their energy, Amy—making them his slaves."

"That's horrible!" She wailed and slid down the wall.

"And he's going to do the same to Ricky. We've got to stop him now." He leaned over her as she sat staring into space. "You've got to help me, before it's too late!" She didn't respond. He shook her. "Amy," he said, pulling her to her feet.

She stood swaying a bit, her face white. Billy supported her in case she fainted. "No, we've, it's—" She looked into his eyes, searching them. "Billy, are you sure?"

He nodded. "But we have to hurry, Amy. There's no time."

She put a hand on the wall and shook her head. "No, there's lots of time, all the time we need." She rubbed her hands over her face and took a deep breath. "Remember? Time is different in your time. It goes slower when you're here."

"Yeah, but he's in danger. I saw him locked in a room. Then, when I fought Dobbins—"

"What! You fought Mr. Dobbins? By yourself?"

"I had to try to save Ricky."

"But, you could have been killed!" she shrieked and then hushed her voice with her hands and looked around. "You can't just attack him," she whispered. "He's powerful."

"Yeah, no kidding." He rubbed his side. "But I had to help Ricky. You've got to help me."

"Shhh." She tried to calm him. "Okay, but how?"

"We've got to work together to defeat Dobbins."

"Where is Ricky?"

"Trapped in a secret room beside the boiler room."

"Show me," she said. Billy grabbed her hand and led her to the boiler room.

In the hallway, he slowed his pace and squeezed her hand when he saw Dobbins walking in their direction. "What are you two doing down here?" Dobbins asked.

"We...we have to get a mop for the janitor," she answered.

"Really?" the headmaster eyed them and pointed his cane at Billy. "And who is he?"

"He's new—just moved from across town," Amy said. Sweat trickled down Billy's forehead.

Dobbins eyed him up and down. "What's your name?"

"Billy, sir."

"Billy what?"

"Billy Maclean, sir."

Dobbins raised an eyebrow. "Have I seen you here before?"

"No, sir." Billy's face heated up.

"Are you related to Arnold MacLean?"

"Ye...Yes," Billy stammered. "He's my grand, ah..." he shook his head, "I mean my cousin." Dobbins tapped his cane on the floor while looking at him long and hard. Billy squeezed Amy's sweaty hand.

"W-we have to-to get the mop n-now, sir," Amy said.

"Yes," Dobbins muttered, still eyeing Billy. "Welcome to Lampson, young man," he said at last.

"Thank you, sir."

"Well, don't just stand there. Get the mop for the janitor. He'll need it sooner rather than later, I suspect."

"Yes, sir," she replied and Billy pulled her forward. Dobbins's cane clicked down the hall and then abruptly went quiet. Billy glanced back as he led Amy to the boiler room. Dobbins stood, staring back at them. Chills ran down his spine just before he pulled her through the door.

He leaned against the wall and shook his head, trying desperately to escape the images still fresh in his mind.

"What's the matter?" she asked.

"I just don't like it in here." He dragged her to the sidewall. "It's like a tomb." Amy gave him a questioning look. "It's the bodies, Amy. Here, look." He swept away some patrol uniforms and turned the doorknob, but it was locked. "Crap, we can't get in without the key and Dobbins has it," he said.

"How do you know that?"

"Because Tommy told me."

"Tommy? Tommy Jenkins?" She shuddered. "He's the first kid who went missing, from Mrs. Bell's class last year."

"His ghost showed me the room and the bodies." Billy shivered.

Amy stared at him for a moment. "I don't want to see that."

"Neither did I," he said, the boys' frozen faces in his mind.

"Tell me how Mr. Dobbins got Ricky."

"It started on Halloween night when I got the Leo back from Andrew."

"What? How did he get it?"

"It fell in the cloakroom, and he picked it up. Anyway, Ricky and I used the force of the lion's head to scare Andrew and his friends away, and we got it back. After that, I figured out Dobbins was after us because when Ricky and I were together, we were stronger."

"What do you mean?" she asked, removing her coat.

"When Ricky and I fought Andrew, we shouted '*Panthera Leo*' together, and the lion's head went brighter and hotter than ever, much stronger than when I did it by myself. It freaked Andrew out."

"Magic is stronger if two magical people use it," Amy said. "But Ricky isn't able to use magic, is he?"

"I think he can, Amy. His mom was able to do magic, but she left when he was little, and Ricky blames the magic for it."

"That explains why he doesn't like me," she said, nodding her head.

"Maybe. The other thing is that I started using spells with the Leo."

"What kind of spells?"

"I tidied my room with it." He smiled.

115

"Cute trick." She smiled back.

"And I saw where Dobbins hid Ricky, and I bet it's in that room." He paused and pointed at the door to the storage area. "Only in the future."

"You mean your time," Amy corrected. "Yeah."

"Wow. How did you get in the room?"

"I escaped Dobbins by using a vortex."

"But you can't access that vortex unless you're in the middle of it. I think that's why I couldn't use it."

"Well, I did—I thought of you, said the words, and bang—I was here."

She gasped. "Wow, that's pretty powerful, Billy."

"Yes, and we have to get in there to use it."

"Okay, but how are we going to stop Mr. Dobbins and rescue Ricky?" She wiped the sweat off her forehead.

"That's why I need you. I'm not strong enough on my own."

"Okay, we'll need to prepare ourselves to fight Mr. Dobbins. He's not just going to let us take Ricky back."

"And what about the bodies?"

Amy shivered. "I don't know. How many are there?"

"Three, so far, and if we don't stop him, there'll be more, starting with Ricky."

"We need to talk to my grandma."

"We don't have time."

"Don't worry. We have time—hold on," she said. "She's not home today anyway, but I've got some spell books we could look at. It's only a few streets away."

"Okay, as long as we hurry."

"When the bell rings, we can sneak out the covered playground door. Nobody will be in there, and if it's clear, we can leave the school grounds."

As if on cue, the bell rang, and Amy started up the steps.

"Wait a few minutes," Billy said, stopping her.

"Why?"

"Let the kids get to their classes first."

"Oh, right," Amy agreed.

After five minutes or so, he opened the door. "All clear," he said, and they darted across the hall, through the covered play area and to the outside door.

Billy opened it slowly. "They're all inside. Let's go." They dashed along the front walk and down the street.

— CHAPTER SEVENTEEN —

Imobilize Eos

"Are you sure about those spells?" Billy asked when they stopped in front of the boiler room
door.

"I'm pretty sure, but Grandma wasn't there to ask," Amy answered. "Do you remember them?"

"Yes, have you got the salt?" He gulped, nerves twitching when they entered the room. The small, dark room brought back the bodies. He shook it off as he looked at Amy, but she did not seem to notice anything.

"Yes."

"Remember, you have to throw it at the right moment," he said, surveying the empty rooms.

"I know," she said.

"Good. Do you have the ocular orb?" He wiped his forehead.

"Of course, it's in my jacket pocket."

"We're ready then," he said, though he felt far from it.

"We can't go until we figure out where the vortex is. Where were you when you fought Mr. Dobbins?"

"Here, in this room."

"Where were you standing when you went through the vortex?"

Billy stepped closer to the patrol slickers hanging to the right of the boiler. "About here." She walked up to him and stopped, shuddering for a moment."What's wrong?"

"Nothing, I'm just sensing the vortex."

"What do you mean 'sensing it'?"

"Well, if you try, you can feel the magnetic pulse of
it."

"Really?" He stepped beside her. "I don't feel anything."

"Try closing your eyes for a second and imagine you're surrounded by energy."

He did what she said. "I still don't feel anything."

"You will. It takes practice. You get goosebumps and feel a little lightheaded."

Billy closed his eyes and focused. "Whoa! My skin is tingling, and my hair is standing on end." He shook as he let the energy flow over him. "This is cool."

"That's the vortex." She paced to the slickers, counting as she went.

"It feels weird." He opened his eyes. "What are you doing now?"

"Measuring the size of the vortex," she said as she moved the slickers aside. "We'll need to get into that corridor for an accurate measurement, but it must be big because it's even stronger here."

"How do you know how large it is?" He gulped when the door to the corridor was revealed.

"On this side, it extends across the room and into the corridor, so if I'm standing at the center of it, I'd have to be in the secret room you told me about because vortexes are circular. That's how you ended up in the corridor in my time, even though you left from the boiler room in yours."

"That makes sense, but how do we know where we'll end up when we go through it?"

"We don't. All we can do is focus on Ricky and hope we land where he is."

Billy pointed at the patrol slickers. "First things first, though. We need to get into that hidden corridor. And I think I know how." Amy raised her eyebrows, following him toward the janitor's office to their right. "Check and make sure no one is coming down the hall. I'm going to look for a spare key." She went up the steps, and he opened the drawers.

He didn't find any keys in the first one, but in the drawer to the right, he found two big rings loaded with them. *Great, it will take all day to figure out which one fits.* He picked up both rings and scurried back to the hidden door. The lock was an old-fashioned kind that required skeleton keys to open. He chose several with the right shape and tested them, but no luck. He had pulled the last key on the second ring out when Amy turned from the door.

"Someone's coming," she whispered, rushing down the stairs. "Hide." She pulled him to some shelves.

Billy, fingers sweating, dropped the last key ring. He bent down to pick it up, but she yanked his arm. "We don't have time." She pulled him behind the shelves.

Billy chewed his fingernails while eyeing the keys in plain sight on the floor. "Someone might come." He stepped out to get them.

Amy grabbed his wrist. "No, wait."

Billy sweated, his heart thumping while they waited for several minutes, which felt like hours. "No one's coming, and we've wasted a lot of time," he said finally, frowning at her.

"Someone was coming." She crossed her arms. "I didn't make it up."

He opened his mouth to argue, but sighed instead. "I'd better put these back and look for some more. Go check the hall again."

Amy nodded, flew up the stairs, and peeked out the door. "All clear." He spotted a ring of keys hanging from a hook behind the desk. He grabbed the keys on the floor, dashed to the janitor's room, dropped them back into the drawer, snatched the other key ring, and darted back to the hidden door. There was a bunch of skeleton keys to check.

The keys slipped from his sweaty hands as he tried them one by one. "Come on, come on," he muttered in frustration.

"Hurry up," Amy said in a loud whisper.

"I know, I know." Billy shook the sweat from his forehead and tried some more.

"The janitor's coming." Amy flew down the stairs, and they hid behind the racks of supplies. Billy clamped his hands around the keys as the janitor, whistling, bounded down the steps, and entered his office. The kids watched while he searched through a bunch of papers on his desk. After a few anxious minutes, he pulled a sheet from the pile, eyed it closely, muttered to himself, and lifted the phone off its cradle. "Yes, it's me. I sent the order last week. Uh-huh...uh-huh... It should be here any day...right, bye." He returned the phone and whistled as he rearranged the things on his desk, grabbed another piece of paper, and dashed back up the stairs and out of the boiler room.

"Make sure he's gone," Billy said, rushing behind the desk. He returned the key ring to its hook and pawed through the shelves, pushing bottles and boxes out of the way and poking through open containers, but he found nothing.

"The key has to be here somewhere," he muttered, looking around, wishing it would jump out of hiding and into his hand. "But where?" He shifted glue bottles and cans of paint on the shelf, flipped open tins and boxes, and shook whisks and towels but had no success. "Where is it?" He raked his hands through his hair, ready to start throwing things.

"Shhh!" Amy said, frowning at him. "Someone will hear you."

"I can't find the stupid key!" He booted an old garbage can. "Hold on. What's this?" Reaching down, he wrestled a dusty, heavy toolbox out of the corner, startled when a black, shiny spider scurried away from it. He knelt down and coughed, brushed away the cobwebs, dusted off the lid, and then pried at the rusty latch. It would not budge. "Come on, you dumb thing." He punched the heavy metal, yanked his fist back in pain, and stood up. Spotting a hammer on the wall, he grabbed it and whaled at the latch, denting it. "Darn it! Open up!" He dropped to his knees and yanked on the latch with both hands. It squealed. He winced, and Amy whined at the sound. Not giving up, he grabbed the hammer again and bashed it a few more times.

"Billy!" Amy whispered loudly, hands covering her ears when he wrenched at the closure. The latch held fast for a second, then gave way with a clunk.

"Yes," he said, flipping the lid open. The smell of grease and paint struck his face as he rummaged through old, rusty tools until he had emptied the top tray. No keys. He groaned and hauled the tray out of the box. Underneath, he raked through more tools. Dust and cobwebs flew everywhere, making him look away and cough.

"Hurry up," Amy said.

Billy wiped his hands on his jeans and stared back into the box. "Uh-huh," he said at last, as several old, rusted keys appeared from under the junk at the bottom of the box. "Here we go." He scooped them up.

Amy peered back at him. "Did you find it?"

"I hope so," he said, sprinting to the locked door. He tried four of them, but they didn't open the lock. "Last one. Here goes nothing," he said, holding up the final key.

"Oh, it better work," she said from the door. "Someone's going to come sooner or later."

The key sank into the hole. Billy held it there a second, afraid to turn it. For an instant, it seemed stuck, so he moved it to the left. Nothing. "It's got to open," he muttered as his slippery hand lost its grip and the key fell out of the lock. "Darn it." He picked it up and shoved it in again, wrenching it to the right. It only went halfway and stuck. "Come on." He grimaced as he twisted it left and then right again. This time, it clicked, and the lock released. The door swung inward, releasing a rush of musty air. Billy gagged, covered his mouth, and turned away.

"What's the matter?" Amy dashed down to join him.

He leaned back, choked, and sat for a moment. "That old room smells awful," he answered, ghostly images of the boys flooding his mind again.

She leaned over him. "It's just old, Billy."

He stared at the open door. "I wish there was another way."

"But you said that was the only way into the room from your time."

Billy straightened up, squinted past the bodies, and focused on Ricky. He pushed their cold stares aside and saw Ricky's face instead.

I have to get past this—got to do it for Ricky! He held onto Ricky's image and sucked air down his throat into his lungs. "Okay, let's go," he said, stepping into the corridor.

Amy followed him, closed the door behind her, and took the orb out of her pocket. "Ready?"

Billy nodded as he focused on Ricky huddled in that bare room. Alone. Amy stared at the orb. *"Oculus me ad spatium futurum."*

A wind from nowhere swept over them, and they entered the vortex. As quickly as it started, the wind stopped, and they struck the floor of a small dark space.

"Ooof !" With the wind knocked out of him, Billy sat up and looked into the dark. "Ricky, Ricky, are you here?" he whispered. Nobody answered.

"Oh," Amy moaned from behind him.

"Are you okay?" Billy asked.

"Yes, I hit my knee on something." Billy heard her fumbling around in the dark. "Oh, my God! It feels like a body!"

"A body. We're too late," he whispered into the blackness.

"Imobilize eos!" someone yelled.

Bam! A blast of white blinded them. *Bam!*

— CHAPTER EIGHTEEN —

The Battle

Billy froze and stared in terror at Dobbins standing against the back wall. Out of the corner of his eye, he saw Amy holding the ocular orb.

"*Regelo!*" she yelled.

The numbness receded from his face, and his limbs melted like sticks of butter as he collapsed to his knees. "Amy." He held his hand out for the orb. "Thanks."

Dobbins raised his cane. "*Congelo!*" A bolt of red crackled from the tip.

Billy jumped to his feet. "*Sicubi incantatores!*" he shouted, deflecting the red bolt into the wall and sending sparks everywhere.

"*Ignis!*" A ball of fire formed in Dobbins's hand. "*Impetum ignis!*" He hurled it at Billy.

"*Agua!*" Billy raised a wall of water, squelching the fire. Steam hissed over him and Amy. "*Tempus et eum!*"

Dobbins wavered and disappeared. "You did it Billy," she said, hugging him.

"Yes, for now, but he'll be back." He leaned against the wall, his hands trembling. "We've got to find Ricky."

"I thought I saw something when Dobbins flashed his spell, but Ricky isn't here," she said, still holding him.

Billy took a deep breath, hands on his knees, and straightened. *Do I have enough strength?* Amy let go of him as he focused on the orb in his palm. "*Lumino!*" Rays of light from the orb lit the room. He could not see Ricky, but he spotted the lion's head lying on the floor. He picked it up. "Take the orb." He handed it to her.

"Maybe Dobbins moved Ricky."

"Or maybe..." He held the Leo up as he said, "*Ricky, ostende te.*" The room shimmered for a second, but instead of Ricky, three ghosts appeared in front of them.

"That's Derek," Billy said.

"And Stephen," Amy said.

"Oh, no, Ricky." Billy's eyes watered. Ricky floated between them, his face blank. Dobbins appeared behind them.

"Too bad about your friend," Stephen taunted.

"He's one of us now," Derek said.

"Shut up!" Billy shouted, anger flooding over him.

Dobbins raised his cane and laughed. "*Draconis impetum!*" Dobbins snarled, and a crimson dragon with fiery wings and teeth like knives sprang from his cane.

Billy's rage rose like a sword. "*Leo impetum!*" he yelled, focusing all of his fury and energy on the spell. A shining golden lion roared and leaped into the air, its claws like razors and teeth like blades. The dragon flapped its wings as it recoiled from the lion's slashing claws. It spewed fire over the great cat, scorching its hide. Billy screamed at the pain running down his own back. Sparks flew, and the acrid smell of smoke filled the room. The king of beasts roared, its razor claws clashing with the dragon's talons. Billy drew the feline back, holding it, crouched and ready to spring.

"*Impetum!*" he shouted. The big cat bounded forward and sliced the dragon's white belly from hip to hip. Dobbins screamed in agony, backing away as the lizard wavered and grew dim. Billy, his back burning, leaned against the wall to catch his breath.

"*Draconis!*" Dobbins shouted. The scaly beast spread its wings and swooped around to claw at the li- on's flank. Pain shot through Billy's side as talons dug deep. He slumped and grabbed his ribs.

"*Regredier!*" Amy shouted. Dobbins pulled back, and the three ghosts around him disappeared.

Dobbins turned to face Amy. Billy pushed off the wall and attacked. "*Leo Impetum!*" The fierce cat sprang forward, raking its claws down the glittering scales, sinking its teeth into its opponent's hind leg.

"*Regredier!*" Amy yelled again.

The dragon screamed fire. Dobbins's image shimmered with the double assault. The tawny beast's shiny mane flashed as its mighty jaws tore at the severed limb and spat it into the air, blood and talons spiraling away. Growling, the fierce cat ripped into the dragon's wing. Dobbins howled, but aimed his cane at Amy.

"*Duratus!*"

"Amy." Billy stared as she froze like an ice statue. The lizard roared fire, singeing the lion's mane. "Agh!" Billy backed away from the burning heat. The beasts circled each other, shimmering, fading, and flashing as they slashed and lunged at each other. Blood and fur flew through the room. He swallowed and shook his head, the ringing in his ears not stopping. The cat's jaws clamped onto the dragon's shoulder.

Dobbins hollered, swayed to the side, pulled away, and screamed, "*Draconis impetum!*" The lizard twisted around, opened its gaping mouth, and sank its dagger-sharp teeth into the lion's belly.

The Leo roared in agony. Billy faltered, grabbed his own stomach, but righted himself, more determined than ever. "*Leo impetum!*" he shouted. The mighty cat, guts spilling out, slashed forward but missed. Dobbins laughed, and the dragon roared, scraped its talons down the lion's back, and bit into the golden fur on its shoulder.

Shrieking, Billy slumped to the floor as the dragon opened its jaws and growled, talons spread to strike the death blow. The golden Leo shimmered and wavered in the air beneath the purple-winged monster. *He is too strong. I cannot do this alone.*

"*Regelo!*" he screamed at Amy. She slumped to her knees, batted her eyes, and raised the orb.

"*Regredier!*" she screamed. Dobbins fell back as if hit by a brick.

"Use the salt!" Billy yelled.

She reached into the bag at her feet. "*Et vade!*" she yelled, throwing the salt.

The dragon and Dobbins disappeared. Billy, drained, lay in a heap. The lion disappeared in a golden shower of sparks as Billy clutched his stomach, sucking in air, heart thumping. Pain throbbed in his side, his face, and his back, but he saw no blood on his hands.

"Are you okay?"Amy asked, crouching down.

It took him a moment to answer. "I think so...but he's too strong," he said between gasps. "We need Ricky."

"But Dobbins has him."

"We need to get him back. Maybe if we focus on him, we can release him."

"I can help you," a voice said from behind them.

"Tommy. I'd forgotten about you." Billy said. "You take care of Derek and Stephen, and we'll release Ricky."

Dobbins appeared again with the three boys surrounding him. Billy, his heart pounding, sweat dripping in his eyes, tried to think of the right spell. He aimed the Leo. *"Ablego Derek. Ablego Stephen!"* he yelled. The two lost boys disappeared. Amy raised the orb.

"Dolor!" Dobbins shouted. Billy doubled over, screaming, intense pain shooting through his chest like a heart attack. He barely held onto the lion's head as the dragon's talons clawed at him on the inside.

"Et vade!" Amy yelled. The orb glowed, and a white dart shot at Dobbins.

"Sicubi incantatores!" Dobbins deflected the light against the wall beyond.

Billy fought through the pain. Ricky floated beside Dobbins, his eyes like circles. *Does he recognize me?* Billy aimed the Leo. *"Liberabis, Ricky!"*

"Ventus!" Dobbins yelled. A blast of wind, like a hurricane, pinned Amy against the wall. *"Detrahere Arma!"*

The lion's head dropped from Billy's hand, and he collapsed, helpless on the floor as Amy struggled to keep fighting. He reached out, grabbed her ankle, and fed her his energy.

*"Desine incantator—"*she started.

"Angues impetum!" A volley of snakes flew at her. Horrified, his body wracked with pain, Billy's eyes raked the

shadows. *Where is the Leo? There. By the back wall.* Keeping his hold on Amy's ankle, he reached for it. Not quite. Amy screamed from behind. He stretched more—still not there.

"*Angues ablego!*" Amy yelled. The hissing stopped. Dobbins yelled. "*Angues impetum!*"

Amy screamed, as the room flashed and the hissing returned. Billy forced his fingers forward a little more, and this time, they just brushed the lion's head. He groaned when it rolled away.

From behind him, Amy shrieked, fighting the hissing snakes. Billy risked a glance over his shoulder to see her swatting at a snake lunging at her face. "*Angues...evanescent!*" she hollered. The snapping viper disappeared.

Billy turned back to the Leo. He stretched further, just as Amy took a step backward, overreaching the head, his hand falling on something else. There was nothing there. He patted the air and definitely felt something. He blinked, but the arm he gripped remained invisible. "Ricky!" he shouted. "Is that you?"

Ricky groaned. Relief washed over Billy as he clasped Ricky's hand.

"*Concedo!*" Dobbins yelled, and a red glow lit the room.

Amy screeched, dropped the orb, and fell on top of Ricky. The lost boys flew over them as Dobbins laughed.

Billy's anger flared. His heart hammered in his chest. He grabbed the Leo and pushed the three of them away from Dobbins with his legs. Braced against the wall, he hauled himself up to his knees and caught a glimpse of Ricky's face, his eyes open. "You're okay," Billy said. Ricky nodded weakly.

"It ends here!" Dobbins yelled as he loomed over them.

Billy rose, faced him, and aimed the Leo. "It ends for you!"

Dobbins's eyes darkened and he raised the cane.

"No more!" Billy shouted. "*Desino!*"

Dobbins laughed. "*Concedo—*"

"*Moriendum est!*" Billy screamed with all his might. The two spells met in the middle of the room. Billy drew all the energy he could from his friends. "*Moriendum!*" The white bolt doubled in size and sizzled forward. It sliced through the red glow and blasted Dobbins into torrents of light. It smashed, splattered on the walls and ceiling, and then slithered along the floor, smoldering and dying like the last embers of a bonfire. Billy collapsed on top of his friends, the Leo held loosely in his hand, as he gulped in air. He gazed at Derek, Stephen, and Tommy, who swirled around them, prodding like worried puppies nosing their sleeping mother.

— CHAPTER NINETEEN —

The Lost Boys

Billy and Ricky caught up with Amy at recess, where she sat by the tall oak.

"Is it really true?" Billy asked.

"They're alive?" Ricky asked.

"As alive as you and me," Amy said. "They're playing right over there." She pointed to the soccer field where the three boys were busy running after a soccer ball and shouting with the rest of their friends.

"How is that possible?" Billy asked, sitting on the nearby rock.

"Well," she started, "first of all, they were never dead." Ricky and Billy gave her a questioning look. "They were under a spell that put them in a kind of suspended state."

"What? Like suspended animation?" Ricky asked, raising his eyebrows.

"I guess so," she said. "It's when you are frozen physically, but you're still alive."

"That's how Dobbins was able to use their energy and control them," Billy said.

"Yes," she agreed. "He was able to command their spirits, but keep their bodies alive."

"Why?" Billy asked.

"Because he could use their energy and control them forever." Amy paused. "Even though his body died, he could live forever, ruling Lampson School."

"What?" Ricky looked puzzled.

"By going after me and you in your time, he'd be even more powerful."

"Okay," Billy said, still a little confused. "But how did they come back to life?"

"Once we defeated Dobbins, their spirits were freed, and they woke up."

"Wow," Ricky said. "Thank goodness."

"Do they know what happened to them?" Billy asked.

"I don't know. They don't want to talk about it."

"Who could blame them," Ricky added.

"What happened to Dobbins?" Billy asked.

"As soon as the police found out what he'd done to the boys, they arrested him," Amy said.

"Good riddance," Ricky said. "Billy, let's get back to the future."

"Sounds good," Billy said, rubbing the lion head in his pocket. "Let's use the vortex in the boiler room."

"See you later, Amy," Ricky said as he turned toward the school.

"Bye, boys. I'll see you in class," she said with a smile.

"Yeah, right," Billy said, smiling back as he caught up with Ricky.

Magic Spells:

Ablego --------------- Send away
Agua ----------------- Water
Angues ablego ------ Snakes, go away
Angues evanescent ------ Snakes, vanish
Angues impetum ------ Snakes, attack
Cella redige ---------- Tidy my room
Concedo -------------- Surrender
Congelo --------------- Freeze
Desine incantators ------ Stop the spell
Desino -------------------- Stop
Detrahere arma --------- Disarm
Dolorem - Pain
Draconis impetum ------- Dragon, attack
Duratus - Freeze
Ego vos perficiam -------- I will finish you
Et vade -------------------- Be gone
Ignis ----------------------- Fire
Ignus draconi ------------ Fire dragon
Imobilize eos ------------ Stop them
Impetum ----------------- Attack
Impetum ignis ------------ Fire, attack
Leo claresco ----------- Lion, light up
Leo impetum ----------- Lion, attack
Leo sistenda ---------- Lion, stop
Liberabis --------------- Free
Lumino ----------------- Light up
Moriendum est --------- You must die
Moriendum ------------------- Die
Oculus me ad futurum ------- Eye, take me to the future
Oculus me ad praeteritum ------- Eye, take me to the past
Oculus me ad spatium futurum ----- Eye, take me to the space in the future
Ostende te ------------------ Show yourself

Panthera Leo --------- Lion
Regelo ------------------ Thaw
Regredier --------------- Back
Sicubi incantatores --------- Deflect the spell
Tempus et eum ----------- Time to send him away
Ubi es, Ricky? ------------ Where are you, Ricky?
Ventus --------------------- Wind

About the Author

Raised in Victoria, BC, Canada, P.N. Holland (Neil) writes in memory of his wife, Kris. He has two children, five grandchildren and two dogs. Neil has taught for over 30 years in Public Schools in British Columbia and holds an M.Ed from the University of Victoria with a major in English. His writing is fast-paced, and his stories are page-turners. Neil also likes to visit schools where he shares his insights on reading and writing with students and teachers alike. Neil is currently working on another trilogy called **Mellissadorha** (**Vahldor** is Book One), a collection of short stories and a detective series.

The Lost Boys of Lampson is the second book in **The Vancouver Island Mysteries Series**. It, and the other books in the series, **The Saxe Point Park Mystery** and **The E&N Escape,** are all magical mysteries with settings close to home. He has written a Teacher's Study Guide for The Saxe Point Park Mystery, which is being used to teach the novel. He is proud of the fact that his book is helping kids improve their reading and writing skills. Neil's books are available in softcover and eBook versions at libraries, bookstores and online (i.e. Indigo/Chapters, Amazon, Barnes & Noble).
Contact https://pnholland.com/ or https://filidhbooks.com for direct purchase options.

Don't miss out!
Visit the website below, and you can sign up to receive emails whenever P.N. Holland publishes a new book.
There's no charge and no obligation.
https://books2read.com/r/B-A-JLFK-MAKEB